WEEKEND IN FARO

Weekend In Faro

A Novel
By
STEVAN V. NIKOLIC

ADELAIDE BOOKS
New York / Lisbon
2022

WEEKEND IN FARO

A novel

By Stevan V. Nikolic

Published by Adelaide Books, New York / Lisbon
adelaidebooks.org

For any information, please address Adelaide Books
at info@adelaidebooks.org

or write to:

Adelaide Books
244 Fifth Ave. Suite D27
New York, NY, 10001

ISBN: 978-1-958419-40-3

Printed in the United States of America

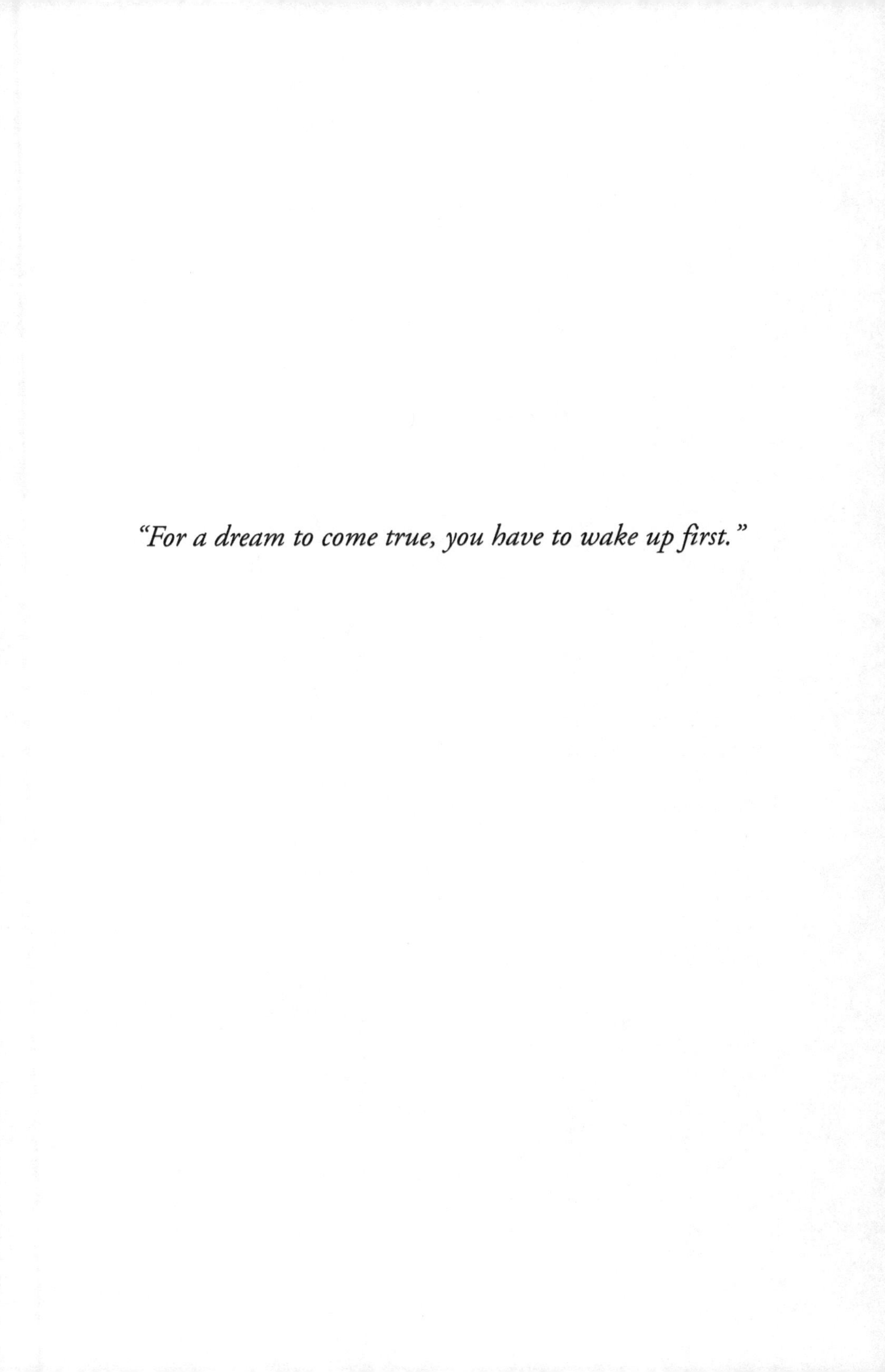
"For a dream to come true, you have to wake up first."

Chapter One
The World of Anu

"Be humble, for you are made of earth; be noble, for you came from stars."—Serbian proverb

In the distant galaxy, many light years away from the planet Earth, exists a world quite similar to our own. It is believed to be somewhere in the constellation of Orion. There isn't a present name for this domain, but old Babylonians were calling it "the world of Anu"— Anu being the main god of the heavenly realms.

Most people don't know that the world of Anu is very important for the inhabitants of Earth. This is a secret that very few know, but from the beginning of time this far away world was in a constant, unbroken connection with our world. The reason is simple: Earth and Anu are two parallel or twin worlds and the same people inhabit both of them simultaneously.

However, there is one major difference between these two domains of existence. On our planet we are born, live, and die in the material world, facing our realities regardless of circumstances, whether they are good or bad, or at least that is the life process we believe. In this other world people live forever in a world of dreams, or as we on Earth would say, in the "virtual world." We are convinced that our lives exist in a material reality—however people on Anu are conscious that they live in dreams. Of course, the world of Anu is not much different from ours except for the fact that everything is a dream.

Some may wonder how it is possible for living beings to be in two distant worlds at the same time. In the dream world there are two kinds of inhabitants: permanent residents and visitors. All of us go to Anu occasionally - that is all of us who dream, but whenever we visit Anu, we are unaware that we are in a world of dreams. A dreamer does not have to be asleep to visit Anu. There are many daydreamers who are able to be awake and at the same time, be in the distant world of dreams. The journey to Anu happens instantly; the moment we start dreaming we are already there.

When it comes to permanent residents of the world of dreams, the story is a bit different. The soul of every living being, including human, has a much longer life span than his carnal body. It usually takes few journeys through many bodies for a single soul to complete its lifetime in the material world. For some souls, unfortunately, it never happens, and they stay forever in the vicious circle of life and death. But those that succeed to complete their journeys continue to live eternal life in the world of dreams.

So, it is not a surprise that from the ancient times until the present, people gaze into night skies towards Orion, trying to find Anu. Every so often we look at the stars saying, "Somewhere there is my true home," without ever realizing why we have that feeling. Many legends were made, stories written, monuments built—all witnessing the efforts of men to secure the successful voyage of their souls into the world of eternal dreams.

This story is about a man name Niki. He was a god-fearing and humble man who lived many centuries ago on the planet Earth. Being a righteous man and a big dreamer, he was often visiting the world of

Anu during his lifetime on Earth, so often, that many residents of Anu thought he was a resident. At Anu, his dreams were always about the same thing—love. But he didn't dream just about any kind of love. His dreams were always about absolute love, the kind of love reserved for gods.

His absolute love was not only the love for a woman. It was about pure and unconditional love for everything that surrounded him: the earth that he walked upon and that gave him fruits, fruits that nourished him; for every plant, flower and leaf; for every living creature that exists from the smallest to the biggest; for air that he breathes; for water that sustains and gives him life; for every human being regardless of origin, race, belief, or station in life; and finally unconditional love for oneself and the eternal joy of being part of that magnificent symphony of creation called the universe.

For a human being it was a daring thing to dream about absolute love and the gods were concerned, but, it was the world of dreams. Everybody had the right to dream anything they wanted. There were no limits. And Niki was a righteous man. It was expected that his dreams would be pure and idealistic. Nevertheless, the absolute love was a divine category not completely compatible with the human kind. So the gods, concerned for Niki's well-being, ordered angels to watch over him whenever he was in the world of dreams. Of course, there was one more reason for the gods' interest in Niki's dreams. There was a slight chance, after all, that men could have the ability of comprehending and living the concept of absolute love. If Niki's yearning for the absolute love was the result of a genetically enhanced transformation and not just an accidental glitch between his mind and his soul without the possibility to duplicate, the potentials for a human kind would be unlimited. Niki could be the beginning of a new race of humans, freed from hate, greed, evil, selfishness, wars and conflicts, poverty and inequality, and all other carnal instincts that humans in their present form possess.

So, after a long and fulfilled life, the time came for Niki to leave the physical world. At the moment of separation of his soul from his body, god spoke to him the words we all hope to hear, "Well done good and faithful servant," and with that, he left. Because he was a good man with a pure soul, his soul was relieved from the circle of life and death and sent to inhabit the world of dreams forever. But something strange happened upon his final arrival to Anu - he didn't want to dream about love anymore.

The souls inhabiting the world of dreams didn't know why. During many visits before, love was all he was dreaming about. But now, when he was finally in the world of dreams and had opportunity to dream such a precious dream forever, he didn't want to do it anymore. There were many speculations about what caused this change in Niki. Some say that a few years before his death on Earth, he met a woman and fell in love, but it was in the physical reality of the material world. The only love that he knew how to share was unconditional absolute love, so of course this love for a woman failed. The circumstances surrounding the events of unrealized love destroyed him. Nothing could bring light to his face and those who knew him believed that he didn't die out of old age or sickness, but were convinced he died from a deep sadness.

As a result, he arrived at the world of dreams without his dream. For a while he was wandering around trying to find a place for his soul. But for that, he needed to dream and the only dream he knew was the one he didn't want to dream. In order to survive, he came up with the absurd solution to steal other people's dreams. Something like that had never happened before in the world of dreams.

On Anu, you could dream about anything without limits and without consequences, as long as it was your own dream. One could dream even of being a thief and steal and never receive punishment because the action only existed in a dream. Yet, to steal other people's dreams was unthinkable. In the world of dreams there were only two rules: 1. Dream your own dreams. 2. Never interfere into the dreams of others.

Events that followed have shaken both worlds and remain registered in the Book of Life forever as a warning—not only to humans, but to gods as well. What follows is the story of what happened.

Chapter Two
Thief of Dreams

"Many things unknown, unwished for, nor ever attempted by our minds, are manifested to us in dreams... which we knew not by any report; and those dreams need not any act of interpretation, which belong to divination."—Cornelius Agrippa of Nesseheim, 1531

When Niki's soul arrived in Anu, all residents that knew him from his previous visits were happy. Finally, Niki would be permanently there and be able to dream his dream forever. They reasoned that as a virtuous man, Niki deserved it. What they didn't know was that his soul was hurting—hurting badly. He was an angry and disappointed man. He was in the world of dreams, but didn't want to dream his dream ever again. Or at least, that is how his soul felt.

Without his dream, his soul was wandering around aimlessly, observing other people's dreams. Oh, there were so many different dreams in the world of dreams. There were good, bad, happy, sad, comic, tragic, peaceful, and violent. People dreamt about everything. Everything was permitted because there were no true consequences. Very often, dreams were about passionate, erotic encounters that lasted for days and nights. Strangely enough, women were more often with such dreams than men. The most common dream for men was about fighting violent battles and winning after killing huge numbers of enemies. Niki could never imagine that somebody would ever enjoy cruelty and dreaming about killing people even if it wasn't happening in reality.

He was confused about many other things he saw on Anu. He always had a perception that the world of dreams was a place for pure and just souls. How was it possible that a pure soul would have impure dreams? He started questioning his understanding of good and evil, right and wrong, true and false. Soon he realized how wrong he had been about many of his assumptions. He felt like he had spent his whole life believing in things that existed only in his dreams. *What a fool he was,* he thought.

And just as he started feeling sorry for himself, he noticed a group of people dreaming that were members of the Illuminati, a secret organization that had been ruling the world. What an interesting dream, Niki thought. He wanted to be in it, but it wasn't his dream. He couldn't just jump into other people's dreams and it was against the rules of Anu to interrupt anybody's dream. Nevertheless, Niki wanted to be a part of it. There must be a way to get in, he thought. What would be the harm? After all, it was just a dream.

And that is when Niki became the thief of dreams without realizing the consequences of his many actions that would follow. For a few days he followed people dreaming about the secret organization, Illuminati. He learned everything he could learn about the dreams the organization had. At the right moment, when nobody was paying attention, he jumped into the dream and became part of it. He did it so well that people dreaming thought his appearance was a legitimate part of their dream. After some time, Niki became a very important leader of the secret organization. Many lives depended on his decisions. He had many servants, many followers, and many responsibilities for the destiny of the world. After all, he was in charge of the organization that was ruling the world from a shadow. What an exciting dream, he thought.

But after a while, he got bored. It just wasn't him. He didn't like secrets. The major problem he had with this dream was the secret association of people dreaming it. Why would anybody who is doing right, want it to be a secret? Something was wrong with this picture. So, Niki decided to leave this dream. And without warning, without giving a notice to anybody, he just disappeared. At first, people dreaming these dreams were confused. There he was, an important part of their dreams, and then, he just didn't exist anymore. Soon, they realized that Niki had fooled them. They saw Niki as a deceiver. They promised revenge, but didn't know the way to do it. They were living in their dreams and the only way to seek revenge would be through the dream, but Niki was no longer there.

His next adventure was much simpler. He came across a man dreaming of opening a chain of bakeries making the best bread and pastries. *I like that idea*, Niki thought. It was an innocent and clean dream, so he jumped into it. He became the head baker in this man's first bakery. They were making wonderful baked goods. Customers were very happy. The business was growing. Soon they opened up more bakeries. The man was so happy with Niki's work that he made him his partner. Things were going well. But then again, Niki got bored and then one day, Niki just picked up and left. His partner was devastated, but Niki didn't care. He was again on the road looking for yet another dream. At the time he didn't know that the only reason he was getting bored was because none of these dreams were his own. He would never be happy in anybody's dream but his.

So there were many dreams that Niki stole while in the world of dreams. He was a father and husband, building a home and raising a family. Of course, he left that one. He was editor-in-chief of a famous magazine. He closed it down. He was professor of history. He was an entrepreneur and investor. He was a pastor of a church congregation. He ran a shelter for homeless people in a big city. He was a lover. He was a con-man and a drifter. He was a king and a slave. He was rich and poor. Regardless of the dream, in every dream that he would jumped in, he followed the same pattern. His arrival into the dream would make a difference. He would always leave his mark and then he would disappear. His disappearance would always cause disturbance and damage to the people in the dreams.

People in the world of dreams started spreading the word about the thief of dreams that goes from dream to dream causing disturbances and it became impossible for angels who were guarding the world of dreams to catch him. Once he was out of a dream, he was invisible. In order to find Niki, angels would have to know the next dream he was going to steal.

Of course, Niki didn't know that what he was doing was a crime. He really didn't feel the consequences of his actions. The moment he would leave any of the dreams that he stole, he completely forgot about those dreams. He also didn't know that angels were already looking for him.

One day, he was walking down a mountain road and after a while, he noticed a long brick wall parallel to the road. He was curious. In the world of dreams there were no fences or walls separating, hiding or protecting anything or anybody. He looked over the wall. It was a huge beautiful garden with all kinds of ripe fruits, blooming flowers, cold streams full of different fish, happy animals running around, birds singing in the trees of the deep forest or flying over blue and clear skies. It was a wonderful picture. *Whose dream was this* Niki was asking?

And then he saw her. He couldn't believe his eyes. She was the most gorgeous woman he had ever seen! Walking in the white and very transparent linen shirt coming just to her hips, with nothing under it, Niki could observe her carefully. She was tiny and very well built. Nothing on her body was too big or too small. Everything was perfectly placed and proportionate; the curves were just right and she carried herself with such a grace. She had light blue eyes, light skin and curly hair falling over her shoulders. Niki guessed she might be in her late twenties or early thirties. Who was she—Niki wondered?

This woman walked through the garden and picked fresh spring flowers. While she was making a bouquet of flowers, it seemed like she was talking to somebody and smiling. But nobody was around her. For Niki, there was something so attractive, so erotic, and so tempting in the way she moved, smiled, and spoke. His body started reacting to his thoughts. He became very excited. He desired to hold that unknown woman in his arms and make passionate love to her. He had to touch her. He had to kiss her. He wanted her to feel him deep inside of her. He had to have her. Whatever it was that she was dreaming about, he would find a way to be a part of it and be with her. Niki jumped over the wall.

Chapter Three
A Beautiful Maiden

"In the material world below, she always felt lonely and there was nobody to understand her true nature. She always kept longing for her true home and could never find it."

Niki wanted so much to get into the dream of this young woman. First, he had to learn everything about her and her dream. As many times before, he was hiding, following a dreamer, and making notes about everything he observed. It was crucial to understand what the dream was all about if he wanted to successfully become a part of her dream. But this one was quite different than anything he experienced before.

For one, he couldn't understand why this dream was happening in the garden that was enclosed with walls. It was so unusual for the world of dreams. Second, it appeared that this woman was constantly with somebody else. Sometimes she was even acting like she was holding somebody's hand, but he couldn't see anybody. Nevertheless, his desire to be with this woman was strong. He followed her for days trying to put together the picture of her dream that would enable him to become part of it. For him, it became an obsession. Each day he spent following and watching her, increased his desire for her.

He carefully studied each and every one of her moves. After a while, he knew many of her habits and routines. He knew what she liked to eat, places she liked to be, flowers she liked to pick and smell, birds she liked to talk to, and when and where she liked to sleep. He enjoyed watching her bathe in the lake in the center of the garden. Oh, he wanted so much to bathe with her, to rub her skin, and to touch her breasts.

But everything he learned in all those days somehow didn't seem enough for him just to show up in her dream. There was still something missing. The more he examined it, he came to the conclusion that the solution was in the invisible part of her dream. But he still didn't understand what the invisible part was. Who was she seeing? Who was with her? Niki knew it had to be a man. Her gentle moves, her smile, the blink in her eyes whenever she was extending her hand to touch this invisible being, told Niki about the affection she felt. It had to be a man. But why couldn't he see this man? This was something that had never happened to Niki before.

He had so much experience with examining other people's dreams, before he would become a part of it. There was never an invisible part. It wasn't logical. It was like having a dream within a dream. Something like that was impossible in the world of dreams. The only assumption that he could make was that if he didn't see this being, she didn't either. But again, it was just an assumption. He couldn't act on that and it felt like he might have to wait an eternity to enter her dreams with her. In the world of dreams time was of no consequence because time did not exist, but his desire for her grew immensely and he couldn't stand to wait anymore.

One morning he decided to show up in her dream based on the little information he had. Niki was confident that the information he discovered while invading so many other dreams would help him if he needed to improvise. He placed himself next to her at the moment she was waking up. She opened her eyes and looked at him.

"Who are you?" she asked.

"It's me," Niki answered. "Don't you recognize me?"

He knew this was a crucial moment. He had to be relaxed.

"But you look much older now," she said. Immediately this comment gave Niki a clue. He was right. It was a man that she was seeing. Niki picked a flower from the ground and offered it to her.

"Take this. This is your favorite flower. Do you remember this flower? Yesterday it was a small bud just sticking out from the ground, and now it's in full blossom. Just like you. Just like me."

She took the flower and smiled. But Niki felt that she was still in doubt.

"Are you hungry? Do you want me to make you something to eat?" he asked.

"Yes, I could eat," she answered, still confused by his presence.

Niki ran around the garden picking up tomatoes and all of her favorite herbs. He knew exactly what she liked. He prepared a wholesome dish. She enjoyed eating it.

"This is so good," she said.

"Of course," Niki said. "I have made this for you so many times and you always liked it."

She smiled again. Niki felt that she was becoming more relaxed with him. It seemed to him that he was playing his role correctly. He was on the right track, but he still needed to prove himself to her. He felt her hesitation. He had to win her full confidence before taking over her dream completely.

"Let's take a walk. It's a beautiful day," Niki said.

"Yes, it is," she agreed.

Niki took her on a walk through the garden. It was the same route she had taken every day. He never asked her for directions; he just walked and she followed. They had a great time talking to birds, animals, flowers, observing the water lilies floating in the pond. Finally, she took his hand.

She started talking. She told Niki how happy she was that they were together. In the material world below, she always felt lonely and there was nobody to understand her true nature. She always knew that she didn't belong to the world of humans. She thought they were all possessive and has limited ways of thinking. She always kept longing for her true home and could never find it.

Niki listened carefully. The picture about her dream was becoming clear to him.

Suddenly, they arrived at a lake.

"Oh, it is time to take a bath," Niki said.

"Yes, I need a bath," she said and began to take off her shirt. Niki started to take off his clothing too.

"What are you doing?" she asked. "You are always doing the same thing. What's wrong with you? You know I am shy and I like to take my bath alone. Stay here," she said in an almost commanding voice, but she was still smiling.

After her bath they went back to the woods in the north part of the garden. There was a small wooden cabin there, which was where she slept. There were just a few pieces of furniture there—a simple bed, table, and two chairs facing a stone fireplace. Soon, Niki realized that according to her dream, he, or the man he pretended to be, was the one who built this cabin for them. So, he continued playing his role. There was only one bed. He was sure they would sleep together. That was all he wanted since he had first seen her.

They were seated in front of the fireplace for hours just talking. For a young woman, she knew so much about art, poetry, and philosophy. She shared her knowledge about gods, souls, love, truth, nature, and the universe. She liked to talk. At moments, Niki, who was himself quite educated, had a hard time catching up with the amount of information she possessed. He enjoyed her wisdom and her way of thinking.

Then, suddenly, she stopped talking, stood up, came over to Niki, sat down on his lap, hugged him and started kissing him. She was rubbing her body on his and he felt the warmth of her vulva on his thigh. Then she took him by the hand and they went to the bed. She undressed herself and then she undressed him. They laid down.

Niki was very experienced in erotic matters and there was almost nothing about a woman's sexuality that could surprise him or especially impress. Yet, what he experienced that night was like nothing he had experienced before. Everything that he knew about women making love was just a bleak unworthy copy of what she gave him. They made love all night.

And if you think that this narrator, or any other narrator after, telling the same story, will go into erotic details of their night together, you are wrong. Not because it is inappropriate or vulgar. There were explicit erotic stories, even about gods making love, and narrators were not shy of sharing them by going into the hottest descriptions. But in this case, there are simply no words that would be worthy of describing their encounter. And if any narrator ever tries to come up with some details, it would be only to arouse the readers' lust, and would not do justice to what happened that night between Niki and the young woman whose dream he invaded. It was just a glorious experience of two bodies melting in one, two souls uniting in one, two hearts beating with the same beat, and two spirits becoming one. Yes, it was a dream.

In the early dawn they got tired and decided to sleep. She pulled his arm placing it under her head saying childishly, "Give me my pillow." She placed one hand on his chest and took hold of the pendant that he was wearing on the necklace around his neck. She fell asleep like that.

Niki was looking at her face, so pure, so innocent, and so angelic. He was wondering about the man that she thought he was. He wanted so much to be that man. He felt like he never wanted to leave her dream. Then, he fell asleep too.

Chapter Four
A Discovery

"Of all the dreams that he could steal, he came back trying to steal his own, which was a crazy notion."

Niki woke up. He opened his eyes thinking about the wonderful night he spent with her. He jumped. He was alone. She was no longer there. He looked around the cabin and couldn't see her. He froze in shock. He recognized the cabin. It was his cabin, the one from his dream. But what was this woman doing there? In his dream, he was with a child, not a woman. He got out of bed and ran out of the cabin still in disbelief. He didn't know who to look for—a woman or little girl? Where was she? he wondered.

Then, he heard a voice behind his back.

"Niki, I got you some flowers. Look!"

He turned and froze again. It was her voice. It was her curly hair, her eyes, and the same white linen shirt she had been wearing all of the time. Now, it was down to the ground covering her feet. She wasn't the grown up woman he spent the night with. She was a small three-year-old girl. It was his Nana, his little flower child from his dream. How had that happened? Something went terribly wrong, he thought.

"Look, Niki. I got them for you. They are called esteva. I have seven of them. Before I picked them, I ask each one for permission. I told them I want them for you. Before I picked them I asked them for forgiveness, just as you told me to do. Aren't they beautiful?" The little girl extended her hand up towards Niki offering him flowers.

He just stood there staring at her and trying to understand what happened. Yes, his heart was pounding from the happiness of being back in his dream, but everything was still blurry. He was confused. This little girl was a girl he had found in his dream when she was just a baby. He had cared for her ever since. Through this child he discovered the meaning of absolute love liberated from all passions, all conditions— love for every living creature, love for nature, and love for the whole of creation. In all the time that he spent refusing to get back to his own dream and jumping from one dream to another dream that were not his, she must have grown into this beautiful woman while waiting for his return. Of all the dreams that he could steal, he came back trying to steal his own, which was a crazy notion. Now, when he was back to himself, time must have turned back, leaving him where he has left off before. *'There is no other explanation,'* he thought. And he didn't mind that she wasn't the young woman from last night anymore. After all, love between him and Nana was not about bodily passions, since she was just a child when he knew her in the material world. It was a completely different love—divine love that only god and a small innocent child could give. Sometimes he truly believed that Nana was a goddess because this little girl taught him what true love was. He was back in his dream. He was happy again.

He dropped down on his knees and started crying. The little girl looked at him with wonder. She started wiping his tears with her small hand.

"Niki, what's wrong? Why are you crying?" Little Nana asked.

"Oh, I was just scared for a moment when I didn't see you in the cabin. It's nothing," Niki answered.

"Niki, Niki, don't worry. Nothing could happen to me. You know that. I am protected. Did you forget? You told me that."

"Yes, I remember now," Niki said, trying to bring himself back to normal. He hugged the little girl. If she only knew how happy he was to be back in his dream—in their dream. He was such a fool for leaving her alone for so long. 'But I will never leave her again, never,' he thought.

"Let's go get some food and make breakfast, Nana," Niki said and he stood up, holding the little girl's hand.

"Yes, but please only vegetables and fruits. And when you pick them, don't rush. You always rush. Ask them first for permission and then for forgiveness for picking them. And only after that, pick them. And no animals and no fish from the lake—they are my friends. I promised them that they are safe with me."

Niki was listening to his little girl and smiling. Her heart was precious and her soul was divine. There was so much love in her for everything around and she was just three years old. She had so much compassion in her. He wished that all human souls could be like that. He loved her so much for who she was.

"But I love fish, Nana. I have to eat fish sometimes."

"No. No fish," she said again.

Niki smiled and said, "Good. You win."

"Of course I win. I always win. I am smart," Nana answered and started laughing. They were laughing together. Yes, she was smart. As a matter of fact, he had always been amazed with the mind of this little girl.

They were walking down the path from the woods leading towards the lake in the middle of the garden. Niki was still in shock from what happened that morning, but he was truly happy to be back where he belonged.

Suddenly, three large figures appeared in front of them and blocked the passageway. They were humanlike but much bigger and with large white wings. The figure in the middle was even taller than other two and had a mark on his forehead in a shape of triangle.

Angels, Niki thought. And the one in the middle must be an archangel. But what were they doing here, in the middle of their dream? And why had they blocked their path?

The archangel addressed Niki, "Niki, you have to go with us."

"But why?" Niki asked. "I am in my dream. I am permanent resident of the world of dreams. And I can't leave my little girl alone. Not anymore".

The archangel told him again in a softer but still demanding voice, "I am sorry, Niki. We are just doing our duty and you must go with us. Don't worry about the girl. She will be safe here in the garden. I give you my word."

"Go with the angels Niki," little Nana said. "Angels are good. They will not harm you. You are under my protection. And I will be here waiting for you."

The angels looked at the little girl and smiled. The archangel lowered his wing and touched her hair. Then he took the mark off his forehead and placed it on Nana's chest. "This is a gift for you." Then he turned to Niki, "Here you have a smart little girl, Niki. You should listen to her. Let's go. We have to go now."

Niki looked at Nana. He couldn't believe that they would be separated again. He still didn't know what was happening. Everything was so confusing that morning. "I will be back fast, Nana. Go play with your little friends at the lake," he said. The angels took him away.

Chapter Five
At the High Council

"We were watching his dream, but not his soul."

Niki was sitting behind the heavy desk made completely out of black glass placed in the middle of the strange space that didn't have walls or a ceiling. Archangel Michael was sitting next to him on his right side. Behind them, two other angels were standing as guards. In front of the desk were three marble steps leading to the podium with nine chairs made from some type of purple crystal. They were aligned in a single row facing the desk with a chair in the middle bigger than those on the sides. On the ground level, on the right side of the podium, was a chair made out of gold.

Niki couldn't see anybody, but in each of the chairs some kind of light was glowing and he felt the presence of entities in the room. 'If I can feel them, but can't see them, they have to be gods,' Niki thought. But why was he there? He still didn't know.

He heard a voice coming from the large crystal chair in the middle: "Niki, you are in front of the High Council of Gods, rulers of all worlds and universes, rulers of all creation, visible and invisible. I am Anu, chief of gods and first among the equal. You are here to answer for the crimes you committed in the world of dreams. Normally, these proceedings wouldn't happen here. As a human soul, you are subject to the will of Yahweh, the principal god of the human kind. During your lifetime on Earth you were a believer in him and the follower of his son, the prophet Jesus. But since your crimes were committed in the world of dreams, it falls into the jurisdiction of the High Council to decide your destiny. It is needless to say that you are the first human soul ever appearing in front of the High Council. So, to allow for the fairness of the process and that you can understand the proceedings, we will conduct this in the form of the human court."

"Here," god Anu continued. "On the left side of our council is seated Yahweh, your principal god, who will act as prosecutor. It is his will and it is within his rights to do so. Your counselor, defending you and talking on your behalf will be Archangel Michael. That was my decision based on the fact that he, as an immortal living being from the line of angels, from whose seeds the human race was created, will be most qualified to explain and defend your behavior. The High Council, nine of us, will come up with an unanimous decision at the end of these proceedings that will decide your destiny. Is this clear to you, Niki?"

Niki wanted to answer, but he was unable to speak. He was opening his mouth, but no sound would come out. He didn't know what was happening. He was scared and confused. Archangel Michael addressed god Anu, "Your Most High Presence, Niki understands. We can proceed."

"Very well,"Anu said. "My Almighty Brother, god Yahweh, will present the charges."

"Your Most High Presence, my Honorable Brothers and Sisters of the High Council" Yahweh started "here we have the human soul that was admitted in the world of dreams, and there committed most grievous and despicable crimes of stealing other souls' dreams, thereby causing suffering to those souls inconceivable in the world of dreams. The list and details of all the crimes I have already submitted to you. Since the beginning of time, when His Most High Presence God Anu created the world of dreams, something like that never happened. Just how deviant this human soul became could be witnessed by the fact that at the end of his crime spree he even tried to enter his own dream as a thief. For such crimes, this human soul deserves nothing less but to be deleted forever from the Book of life and more than that—I will make sure that his earthly presence that he already completed, will be deleted as if he never existed. He deserves nothing less! More so, if we don't punish this human soul in this manner, it will be a big embarrassment for all of us in the eyes of the souls residing justly in the world of dreams. I have spoken."

"Very well," Anu said. "Do any of the Honorable Brothers or Sisters have to say or ask anything before I give word to the counselor?"

"I have a comment, Your Most High Presence," goddess Nabia said. "From the material submitted to us, I could see that this soul came to the world of dreams with a very particular dream of absolute love. It is a divine concept, strange to humans and hard for them to comprehend. As a follower of the Yahweh, the only place he could get the ideas of the absolute love was in the teachings of Jesus Christ, son of Yahweh. So whatever happened to him upon final arrival in the world of dreams that made him become a thief of dreams, must have been connected with his earthly beliefs. I don't care much about what will happen to this human soul, but I am offended by the statement of Honorable Brother Yahweh saying that not deleting this soul would be an embarrassment for all of us. It would be an embarrassment only to him, for tempting humans to try to comprehend such a precious concept."

"My Honorable Sister Nabia," Yahweh said. All of my believers on the earth were promised salvation through the acceptance of blood from the sacrifice of my son, Jesus Christ, who died for their sins on the cross. His teachings about love are not of any consequence here."

"So now, on the example of this poor soul, you are denying your own son's teachings, if I understand correctly?" Nabia asked.

Yahweh wanted to answer, but Anu stopped him. "My Brothers and Sisters, this is not the place nor the time for a quarrel. Let's see what our Counselor has to say. Archangel Michael, give us your word."

"Your Most High Presence, Most Honorable members of the High Council, Almighty Yahweh," Archangel stood up and started. "Here we have Niki, poor human soul that was so pure and righteous during its earthly life, that it gained access to the world of dreams only after one circle of life. That in itself is rare and commendable. Even during his earthly life, he was so often a visitor to the world of dreams that everybody thought he was a resident already. The same is happening now to his female counterpart, who is still in the world of living, regularly visiting the world of dreams. Yes, I mention his female counterpart. That is where the cause of all of Niki's problems began. We know that his dream was of absolute love, which is a divine concept conditioned by the duality of the souls of gods. In human conditions, where souls don't have that ability, absolute love could be realized only through the unification of two identical souls, one male and the other female, into one. It is almost impossible to happen, but it did to Niki. In the world of dreams, Niki was fortunate to find his counterpart, even during his earthy existence. In his dream, she was a three-year-old girl. He was twenty-three. Of course, this was acceptable because the absolute love of souls has nothing to do with physical passions of humans, but there was a problem. Both of them were still living in the material world on Earth and getting older there. Niki always felt a presence of his female counterpart on the earth. Close to the end of his life, his longing became so strong, that he started searching for her in order to unite in the absolute love on the earthly level. Of course, at the time, that would be possible, because she grew up into a mature and beautiful woman. At one point, he thought he had found her, but it was a mistake. It wasn't her. It left him hurt and disappointed and then, shortly after, he died and came to the world of dreams."

"Here, in the world of dreams," Archangel continued, "Everybody was impressed by the human souls who are able to achieve absolute love. It was the example of the success and greatness of our creation. Nevertheless, god Anu was still cautious about the progress of the human souls, so he ordered a wall to be built around this dream and angels to be posted as guards, so it could be protected and observed for the benefit of the future development of human souls. So we angels were there, waiting for Niki to show up in his dream. His female counterpart was still visiting regularly, but Niki never came. He was hurt, and upon arrival to the world of dreams, he denied himself to dream the only dream that he had in his soul. By doing that his soul became empty. And nobody noticed that. We were watching his dream, but not his soul. His empty soul started jumping from dream to dream, never realizing its true identity, never truly happy—just making disturbance and damage. An empty soul, my Honorable Gods, can't be responsible for its actions—we all know that.

At this point, Archangel paused, and then he said, "It was only by accident or when drawn to his own dream, we would never know, that he jumped over the wall of the garden, trying to steal his own dream. Not realizing what was he doing, he got noticed by my angels, and soon after he was apprehended. In the meantime, after uniting with his female counterpart, his dream took over his soul again, and he was again Niki, that pure human soul that everybody respected in the world of dreams."

Archangel paused again before continuing, "So, now, my Honorable and Almighty Rulers, I ask you: Who is responsible for what happened? Is it Niki, for trying to find the absolute love in the material world? Is it god Yahweh, for permitting his son Jesus to teach humans about love? Is it Angels, for not noticing an empty and hurt soul arriving into the world of dreams? Is it the gods, for allowing this experiment in divine love between human souls to happen in the world of dreams? I apologize for taking liberty to say this, but we all have a part in the responsibility for what happened to Niki—all of us. So, the only solution now is to let him go back to his dream and we may still see the success of this story. What happened was a mistake. We may learn from it for the benefit of the future of human souls and not punish one human soul that made a realization of the concept of absolute love that had been available and possible only to gods. God Yahweh wants this soul deleted and I ask you, if we do so, what will happen to its female counterpart? She is still among the living, as pure and righteous as Niki was. She is still visiting the world of dreams and dreaming the same dream. Right now, she is waiting for Niki's return to their garden. Does she deserve to be punished with eternal loneliness, just because she dared to dream of the absolute love? I have spoken, " Archangel said and sat down.

"Well, that was a lengthy discourse, Counselor," Anu said. "We appreciate your diligence. Do any of the members of the Council have a question or a comment before we retire to make our decision?"

"I do." Goddess Nabia asked for a word again. "I just wanted to thank Archangel Michael for spreading more light on this unfortunate happening. It will certainly aid in making up my mind."

"We will now retire to make our decision," god Anu said, and the glow of the lights in the nine chairs disappeared. The gods left.

Chapter Six
The Judgment Day

*"But I will punish you according to the fruit of your doings,
saith the LORD: and I will kindle a fire in the forest thereof,
and it shall devour all things round about it."*
—Jeremiah 21:14

Niki was looking at Archangel, while still in disbelief that this was happening to him. He had a remembrance of his misdoings before coming back to his dream, but he couldn't comprehend the depth of his guilt, especially not now when he was finally back in his dream. He didn't care about his destiny anymore. All he cared about was Nana. What will happen to Nana?

He felt the cold stare and presence of the god Yahweh. As a prosecutor, he could not participate in the council deliberations. *'He wants me deleted. How ironic that is,'* Niki was thinking, *'that for all of my earthly life I believed in this god who now wants to destroy me. To whom can I pray to now?'*

Niki didn't know how much time had passed, but the glow of the lights suddenly returned to all chairs. The High Council was back.

"Niki," he heard the voice of the god Anu. "We have made our decision. Your soul will not be deleted. We couldn't come to the unanimous decision on that proposal. One of the members of the Council was too stubborn to budge."

Archangel Michael smiled. He knew it was goddess Nabia.

"But, also," god Anu continued, "You will not return to your dream now. You will have to pay for your crimes first. So, your soul will be send back to Earth, in the body of the living man, and there you will suffer to live through all your crimes again, each one of them. And if you survive them and do not end up dead or in jail for life, you will be able to search again for your counterpart in the world of living. If you find her and she accepts you there, your soul will be pure again. You will be allowed to return together with her to the world of dreams and your souls may live on in your dream forever. This is our decision. Counselor, do you have anything to say on behalf of this human soul before I close proceedings?"

Archangel stood up. "Your Most High Presence, Honorable members of the High Council, this is not a just decision. Returning Niki to Earth to go through all his crimes again in the material world would be a death sentence for him. He would never survive it. The world of living is not a dream world. Those who would want to revenge and punish him for his crimes would multiply in numbers with each crime and he would not have a place to hide or a person to turn to for help. God Yahweh certainly won't help him. And even if, by some luck, he survives, his memory would be completely deleted by entering into another human body, so he would never remember his dream. And even if he does remember and finds his female counterpart, his soul would be so tainted with his crimes, that it is a question of whether or not she would ever recognize him and accept him. As a matter of fact, we can't even be sure if she would recognize the true Niki or the thief who tried to steal her dream. And lastly, where would be the point of time that Niki would be returned to? Who would he find? If we send him back in time, he would have the chance to find his counterpart as a child or as a woman. But if we send him into present time, by the time he pays for all his crimes, his female counterpart may depart the world of the living or she may be very old. With all of those obstacles, your Most High Presence, this is a death sentence for Niki."

"Yes, we thought about the memory loss problem," god Anu said. "That question was raised by Honorable goddess Nabia too. And we have a solution. If Niki survives suffering through all of his crimes on Earth, you will, Counselor, at that moment, be allowed to visit Niki on Earth and remind him of his true nature. That would enable him to sense his female counterpart and to search for her. When and if he finds her, the question of her recognizing him and accepting him is not in our domain. It is between two human souls. After all, we are talking here all day about love, aren't we? And the last one, the question of the time lapse, we will have to leave it to a chance. For absolute love, there should not be time limits. It is eternal."

"With this our proceedings are closed," god Anu said.

Moments after, Niki remained alone in the dark.

Chapter Seven
Crossing Over

"He didn't want to tell him that he was for years a captive of his own dreams, chasing after something that he couldn't know if he would ever find or if it even exists at all."

Over six feet-tall, slim, dressed in skinny Levi's jeans and slim fit Massimo Dutti white cotton shirt, Michael Nicolau would look much younger than fifty-five if not for his short cut grey beard, mustache and hair. He lost lots of hair in his early age and what was left, he kept very short. For his age, his face was pretty smooth with few wrinkles that would intensify only when he was very tired. He was very agile and kept in shape with long walks. With deep, dark brown eyes and a mystic smile, he was a charmer who knew how to fit in, in any group and participate in any conversation, particularly when it came to women.

"Mister Nicolau, mister Nicolau—"

Michael opened up his eyes. There was a stewardess touching his shoulder while saying, "Mister Nicolau, we are about to land in Lisbon. Please, fasten your seatbelt and put your seat in the upright position."

Michael looked at his watch. The plane was arriving in Lisbon earlier than he had expected. He hoped that Carlos was already waiting for him there.

§

Michael knew Carlos for many years. They were both Freemasons, both antique book collectors and shared common interests in various esoteric teachings. Carlos respected Michael for his knowledge in esoteric sciences and was one of very few friends who never judged any of Michael's mischiefs. Nevertheless, there was a big difference between these two men. Contrary to Michael, who almost never completed any of the goals in his life, Carlos was a well-established medical doctor, professor at a university, and a writer.

"Olá Michael! Welcome to Portugal," Carlos said, and hugged his friend when Michael walked out of custom control at the airport.

Like Michael, Carlos was in his fifties. He was a medium height, slightly overweight, strong black hair with almost no gray, big blue eyes, tan skin, clean shaved, and with almost perfect facial lines. Carlos was a handsome man. He always dressed in meticulously fitted designer suits, with his routine straight posture, giving off the impression of an authoritative, wealthy man.

"Hi, Carlos. I'm really happy to see you. Finally, I got to Lisbon. We have been talking for years that I should come and visit."

"Yes, but I know that you would not come if you were not going to Faro. Anyway, it is good to see you even for an hour. I was wondering what happened to you after you broke your affiliation with the Grand Lodge of Freemasons back in New York. You never called, never wrote. I heard many bad things, but I never paid attention to those rumors. "

"Oh well," Michael said, "People like to talk about others when they have nothing smart to say about themselves."

Carlos drove Michael to the Lisbon Oriente train station. There was still about two hours before the train to Faro, so they sat in the café and spoke about the times they spent together searching for rare medieval manuscripts or how they discussed arcane books in the Grolier Club. Carlos knew about the conflict that Michael had with some Freemasons in New York. He also knew about the bad investments that Michael made in publishing and the debt that he had accumulated over the years, thanks to his failing business endeavors, but he didn't mention any of it.

Finally, he asked, "So, Michael, what really brings you to Portugal? You mention this book by a Portuguese author that you want to publish, but that doesn't seem too convincing to me. What are you up to, my old friend?"

"It is about a book, among other things. But you are right, that is not the main reason. It is about the author. I want to meet her in person. We met online accidentally a few months ago and started communicating. She is a very interesting person. Not only does she have an exquisite mind, but she is also good looking. I don't know exactly why and how it happened, but we became attracted to each other. Everything happened so quickly over distance, online. I know it sounds crazy, but I need to see her in person, to spend some time with her, and to figure it out."

Of course, Michael didn't want to tell Carlos about his strange dream and his mission. He didn't want to tell him that he was for years a captive of his own dreams, chasing after something that he couldn't know if he would ever find or if it even exists at all. That "something" made him leave his family and friends, destroy his marriage and his business, and it almost cost him his life. It was an obsession that he couldn't control. Sometimes, he would have the urge to get up and search for it. He didn't know where to search, but for the last few months some strange voice was echoing in his brain, telling him over and over again, "Go to Portugal. She is the one." So here he was.

On the other side, Carlos and everybody who ever met Michael, knew that he was an incurable dreamer. He always aimed for goals and ideals that were hard to be realized in the material world. Somehow, he always managed to make his dreams become a reality, but almost always, once he reached his goal, he lost interest in it and would turn to something else. So, people admired him for his ability to achieve almost anything he put his mind to, but they also perceived him to be an unstable person that doesn't always know what he wants.

"Yes, I suspected it was something like that," Carlos said. "It is so typical of you. I've known you for years and there is only one thing that is constant in your life. You keep chasing dreams. And I admire you for your persistence, but as your friend, I have to give you a word of caution - for a dream to come true, first you have to wake up and then stay awake. And I give you credit for your ability to turn your dreams into reality, but somehow, you never learned how to maintain them that way—how to stay awake with both feet on the ground. I just hope you know what you are doing. You are not a kid anymore."

"Yeah, I know what you mean. My life resume is not so commendable. I messed up so many things over the years, but I think I am finally on the right track. You don't have to be concerned."

"Hmm, isn't that exactly what Chris Corleone, god bless his soul, told you just a day before he killed himself?"

"Don't worry Carlos. I am not losing my mind. And I am not Chris."

"Anyway, what happened to Chris's book collection after his death?'

"I helped his wife sell them to Madison Avenue Rare bookstore. She received a substantial amount. She had enough to cover his funeral expenses and pay off his loans."

Soon it was time to get on a train. Carlos helped Michael find the right train car and brought his luggage to the train.

"Michael, be well and have a safe trip. Anything you need, you know my number. Give me a buzz. And let me know how things are going. Don't be a stranger. Okay?"

They hugged and Carlos left.

Chapter Eight
Chris Corleone's Secret

"...these books have their own integrity, their own identity. It is not about the words in there. You don't need to read these books. Words are there to confuse you. They are just messing around with your mind. You have to look beyond words."

Michael jumped. It was 5:15 p.m. The train was arriving in Faro at 5:35 p.m. He had to take down his luggage from the overhead compartment and prepare to get off the train. The last three hours passed so quickly. The conversation he had with Carlos made him think about their mutual friend Chris who died ten years ago. He hadn't thought about him for many years, but he spent the whole train ride thinking about Chris. It upset him that Carlos compared him to Chris.

Chris was a peculiar character. He was in his late forties, with strong, but already completely gray hair and he was always unshaven. He looked much older than he really was. He was of medium height and build, with a belly sticking over his waist line, and a strong eastern European accent. He always wore a black worn-out suit and white shirt without a tie. Upon first sight, everybody would think that he was an Orthodox Jew who came to New York from Russia, but he was Polish, from Gdansk. At least, that's what he was telling people. His full name was Christopher Antonio Corleone; nothing Polish about his name. But he never bothered explaining the origin of his name. For him, there was nothing unusual about being Polish with an Italian name.

He lived in Greenpoint, Brooklyn. It was, at the time, predominantly a poor working class Polish neighborhood. His wife worked at the counter in a local Polish butcher shop. Chris never worked, or at least, nobody knew if he ever worked. Nobody knew his occupation or if he ever had one. Nobody knew what schools he finished or if he ever finished any.

But in the world of antique and rare book collectors in New York, everybody knew Chris. That is where Michael met him. He was one of the most passionate rare book collectors Michael had ever met. Of course, like all rare book collectors he had his special field of interest. Chris was obsessed with antique and rare books on occult subjects.

Being a rare books collector is a very expensive hobby. Very few people have enough money for it. But somehow Chris was able to come into possession of some of the rare and most expensive titles on the subject. In his collection he had over five hundred books. Many of them were the only remaining copies of books and that is another thing about him that nobody knew; how was he able to do that?

However, for Michael personally, the most fascinating thing about Chris was that he never read any of his books. How did Michael know that? Well, he was the one reading them. Chris would often call him to examine books that he wanted. Michael's job was to read through the book and tell him in short what it was about and why it was significant. Then, Chris would take the book, hold it in his hands, turn it around, and look at it from all sides, like it was a rare piece of jewelry. It seemed like he was trying to feel the book. Then he would open it slowly, running his fingers softly over the pages, examining illustrations, sometimes, even smelling the paper, and only then would he decide if he was going to buy it. It was a ritual. Michael's reward was to read books and copy those that he was interested in. So, it worked well for both of them.

There were a few times, Chris gave books to Michael that he didn't want or he would just buy books that Michael wanted for himself. Once, there was this book dealer offering the rare 1881 edition of Three Books of Occult Philosophy by Cornelius Agrippa. They went together to meet the dealer. The book in itself was insignificant, if not for the notes in it. Originally, Aleister Crowley owned it and he wrote his notes on the margins of the pages. The dealer was offering this book for a very reasonably price of two thousand dollars. Michael was really excited about the notes that Crowley made in the book. Chris took the book, looked at it for a while and then he said, "I don't want it." Michael was furious. He told him, "Chris, these are notes by Crowley. Do you know how valuable this is?"

"I don't care about Crowley," Chris said. He was ready to leave. Michael was holding that book in his hands and he couldn't believe what Chris had just said. Then, Chris looked at Michael and asked, "Do you like it?" He answered, "Yes, of course I like it." Chris put his hand in his pocket, took out a roll of hundred dollar bills bound together with a rubber band, counted two thousand and gave it to the dealer.

"It is sold," he said. He looked at Michael saying, "It is yours. Are you happy now?"

Michael couldn't believe what Chris just did, but he didn't refuse it. He really liked that book.

Everybody in the society of bibliophiles in New York knew about the way Chris was examining books. They all believed that he had some special ability to sense the authenticity of the books. Once in a while some really good copies or fake books would be offered on the market, and dealers, knowing his ability, would call Chris to give an opinion. Of course, he would always use Michael to assist him. Chris would take a book in his hands and hold it for a while. If it was fake, he would tremble with his hands and sometimes with his whole body until he dropped the book. It was a good enough sign. Regardless how many times experts would try to prove the opposite, his feeling was always right. And nobody knew how he did it.

His unique ability to recognize counterfeits didn't stop people from the bibliophilic community in New York to make fun of Chris. He was, as they used to say, "rough around the edges." At the regular meetings in the Grolier club, they were usually discussing rare books and the art of bookmaking. Chris was always there, but he would never say anything. He would just sit in the corner of the room. After a few hours, he would look at Michael and say out loud so everybody could hear, "Michael, how can you listen to these idiots. Let's go to a bar in East Village and find some pussy to fuck. We'll learn more from them than from these mummies."

Michael didn't know why he liked Chris, but he did. Chris was nothing like him. Michael had been researching metaphysics and esoteric teachings for many years. Books that Chris collected were a great source of knowledge for Michael. For Chris it was different. Michael didn't see that as unusual. People collect all kinds of things. There are stamp collectors, coin collectors, and they don't spend that much time thinking about what is behind the things they collect. They just like it. So, for Michael, it was the same with Chris—it was just that he collected books. A few times he asked Chris about what it meant for him to have those books. He knew that Chris wasn't reading them. Chris would just look at him and say, "Michael, these books have their own integrity, their own identity. It is not about the words in there. You don't need to read these books. Words are there to confuse you. They are just messing around with your mind. You have to look beyond words. There is a big secret somewhere in these books and I am going to find it. And you know that, but you are afraid to admit it. It is dangerous."

Well, Michael heard many times this statement from people interested in esoteric teachings, so he didn't pay much attention to these words. In the world of those searching for a deeper meaning of life, there is always a secret that they are after, and it always seems within their reach. He thought Chris is just one of those lost souls trying to find himself. That is to say, he thought that until one October night nearly ten years ago.

It was just past midnight when Michael's phone rang. It was Chris. He was very excited. "Michael, I found it," he said. "I know the secret."

"What are you talking about?" Michael asked.

"Michael, it is all here. It is clear. And you are here. You know that you are at the top, don't you? You are the King, man. The King! Ha, ha, I knew there was a reason I was hanging out with you." He was laughing.

"Chris, I don't understand a word you are saying," Michael said.

"Oh, you know, you know. Listen, I am calling you to tell you I have to go home now. It is time for me.

"Where are you going? Are you going to Poland?" Michael asked.

"No, man, no. I am going home, my true home. Listen, I just wanted to tell you that I am sorry I won't be with you when you go through. But remember, the trick is in the eighth door. It is glass door, the one before the last. You will get out on seventh door tired and you will see the ninth door through the glass of the eight. You will think it was an easy step. But the eighth door is a revolving door. If you get there and think about words, you will get caught, and roll around forever until your mind gets completely lost. Just close your eyes and go straight through. Don't think about words. Remember!"

Michael was holding the phone thinking, *'what just happened?'* Too much polish vodka, he thought. But he never saw Chris drunk before. He thought about calling him back, but he didn't. Then he went to sleep.

Next morning, Michael was in his office already having his second cup of coffee when the phone rang. It was John Robinson from the Grolier Club.

"Michael, did you hear about Chris?" he asked.

"No. What about Chris?"

"Chris was on the news. He jumped off the roof of his building early this morning."

"Chris? You mean Chris Corleone?" Michael asked.

"Yes, man. Your buddy, he killed himself," John said.

Michael couldn't say anything for a minute. He was thinking about that phone call the night before.

"Michael, are you there?" John asked.

"Yes, I am just shocked. I spoke to him late last night. He was excited about something, but he didn't sound depressed."

"Well, whatever happened, happened. It was unfortunate. He always seemed strange and unstable to me. God knows what brought him to the edge." John kept talking. "But he had a valuable collection. Dealers are going to rush there to get whatever they can. He was your friend. Maybe you should help his wife handle it."

"Yes, yes, of course." Michael said. But he was still thinking of his words from last night. He just didn't know what it was that Chris was talking about. "Yes, I will go to his home today. I have his address. Thank you for calling, John." Then he hung up.

Michael took a cab to Greenpoint, Brooklyn. He knew where Chris lived, but he had never been in Chris's house. When the cab arrived there, Michael looked at the building with surprise. It was not a house. It was a rundown four-story brownstone building. In front of the building on the left side of the entrance there was still yellow police tape around the spot where Chris fell. That part of the sidewalk was covered with blue plastic. Michael walked to the entrance and looked at the buzzers. It was supposed to be apartment 2A, but the name on it wasn't Corleone. The name was polish: Wojchek. He pressed the buzzer anyway. The doors sounded and he pushed them open just enough to find himself in the dark hallway with just one light bulb working. It was the kind of building that he would never walk into if he didn't have to. As he was walking up the stairs to the second floor he was thinking how ironic life was. Chris's book collection was probably worth much more than the whole building Chris lived in. He walked to the door of the apartment. It was wide open and he could hear voices.

He walked in. The living room was full of Polish people whispering. The room was very simple and poorly furnished. The only piece of furniture that was sticking out was a huge wooden book cabinet with tight glass doors and the cooling unit next to it that was maintaining the temperature and humidity of the cabinet. Chris's collection was there.

At the far end of the room four women were seated on the sofa. The woman seated in the middle was crying while trembling and talking in Polish to herself. *'She must be his wife,'* Michael thought. He felt confused. He couldn't say good morning. There was nothing good about the morning. He didn't know how to start.

"I am a friend of Christopher's." Everybody stopped talking. The woman raised her head and looked at him. He will never forget that look. It was full of hate.

Then, she screamed at Michael with a broken voice, "I know who you are. You are a devil! You came to get my Andrushka's books! Take them! I don't want them in my house! They killed him! They killed my Andrushka! You killed him! Get out! Get out!"

Michael was standing there not knowing what to say. He didn't know why she was calling Chris, "Andrushka." He didn't know why she was referring to him as a devil. Then, an older man in his sixties approached Michael.

"You are Michael Nicolau, aren't you?" he asked.

"Yes, I am," Michael answered.

"Chris was telling me about you. Come with me into the next room." He pulled Michael to a bedroom. It was the only other room in the apartment. A queen size bed, wardrobe closet, two night tables and a chair were the only furniture in the bedroom. A big crucifix hung on the wall over the bed and a wedding picture on the opposite wall. The bed was still not made and there was an open book on one side of the bed.

"Mister Nicolau, please forgive my sister. Lena is still in shock. We all are. We are all trying to understand," the man said.

"But what happened? Can you tell me, please?" Michael asked.

"Well, he was sitting all night in the bed with this book that is still here." He pointed at the open book on the bed. "And this morning, around six, when Lena woke up to get ready for work, he was still in the same position, siting with the book. She went to the bathroom and when she came back, he wasn't here. Then she heard screams from the street. She looked through the window and she saw him lying on the sidewalk in his pajamas in a pool of blood. Witnesses who saw him told police that he just walked off the roof. He didn't jump. He just walked off. Nobody knows why."

"I am so sorry," Michael said. "I never thought that Chris would do anything like that. He always seemed very stable and full of life."

"Mister Nicolau, it is kind of you to say that, but there is no need. Chris was a troubled man. It is tragic to say this, but maybe Lena will have some peace now."

Michael didn't expect a comment like this. He didn't know how to answer. Then he looked at the book. He recognized it. He was with Chris when he bought it. It was a good buy. It was Gabriel Rolenhagen's, *Selectorum Emblematum Centuria Secunda* from 1613. Original edition, very rare. It was open on the page with one of Michael's favorite emblems, called "In se sue per vestigia volvitur."

"And you say he was reading this book all night?" Michael asked.

"Reading?" Man asked, surprised. "No, Sir. He was staring at this picture all night. Chris didn't know how to read or write. He was illiterate. He and Lena came from the small village near Gdansk thirty years ago. He never went to school. Chris signed his citizenship papers with the print of his palm. But he never wanted anybody to know that, especially not your rich friends. He always wanted to be different. He came here as Andrey Wojchek. At the beginning, things were ok. But then he started with these books. Nobody knew why. Then he legally changed his name. When I asked him why, he yelled at me that it was his true name. He tried to work different jobs, but he could never hold to them for more than a month or two. Most of the time they were living of Lena's paycheck from week to week. Any money that he would get, he was spending on books. When he had no money, he was borrowing around until he couldn't borrow anymore. Then he would sell some of his books, repay a little bit of debt and buy more books and then he would borrow again. It was a vicious circle, a nightmare. If I could only tell you how many times they were evicted from apartments for not paying rent, or how many times the electricity or phone was cut off, you wouldn't believe it, Sir. And now, Lena doesn't have money even for a funeral and he left her with so much debt."

Michael looked at him trying to understand if they were talking about the same man. But again, many things about Chris were becoming clearer to him, many details that he didn't pay attention to before. But the fact that one of the most passionate rare book collectors in New York was actually illiterate was mindboggling to him. How could he not see that in all those years he spent with Chris?

In the following days, Michael helped Lena's brother sell Chris's book collection to a Madison Avenue Rare Book Dealer. He even included books that Chris gave to him—even the one with Crowley's notes.

Lena got enough money to pay for the funeral and pay back all of Chris's debts. There was enough money left for her to put her life together.

A year later, Michael stopped by the butcher shop she was working in to say hello, but she didn't want to talk to him. She just turned her face. Michael walked out. He never saw her again.

Soon after, Michael got divorced. To settle with his ex-wife, he sold his own book collection to a book collector in Iceland. In turn, the buyer donated Michael's collection to the local library under the condition that all of the books always stay together catalogued under the name "Michael Nicolau Library." The buyer was a man who respected Michael's work in the field of esoteric sciences and he wanted to honor Michael with this gesture. On other hand, Michael was pleased that his work would be remembered and preserved somewhere. That was the end of Michael's antique book collecting career. He never went back to the Grolier Club.

He forgot about Chris almost all together. Life went on. He worked in publishing with ups and downs, but at least, he was working with books.

Chapter Nine
Santa Maria Hotel

"It was an obsession. You were chasing your dreams. It is still an obsession and you need to get out of it. For your own good."

The train pulled into Faro train station and stopped. Michael walked out looking for the station exit. There must be some taxi out there, he thought. It was early January, but an unusually warm Thursday evening. The weather was in contrast to cold, windy New York which was covered with snow when he left that morning.

The station was full of tourists from England and Germany. Faro, with its mild Mediterranean weather and beautiful beaches, sitting on the southern coast of Portugal is a popular destination for tourists from northern parts of Europe.

"To Hotel Santa Maria," Michael said to cab driver as he got into the taxi.

The hotel was just a few minutes' drive from the train station. It was one of the oldest hotels in Faro situated in the center of town. Michael chose that hotel because of the name. He thought of it to be symbolic. He was going to be in that hotel with a woman he loved whose name was Maria. It was also the ancient name of Faro. Up until the ninth century, when Moors conquered that part of Portugal, Faro was known as Santa Maria.

"I booked a room for two," Michael said to the receptionist at the hotel.

"Do you want a room with two single beds or one double bed, the receptionist asked.

"One double bed, please."

The young woman at the reception desk said, "Very well, here it is. Let me print the invoice and get you the keys. And the second person is arriving...?"

"Oh, my friend is arriving tomorrow night," Michael said.

§

Michael woke up tired on Friday morning in the hotel room. He dreamt about her again. She was lying next to him, touching his ears with her fingers, holding his medallion in her hand, pulling his arm to make a comfortable resting place for her head. She placed her leg over his and then she disappeared. It was a beautiful dream. Again.

The phone rang. He picked it up.

"Mr. Nicolau, there is long distance call for you," the voice on the other side said.

"Okay. Put me through, "he answered, wondering who was calling at this time.

"Hi, sweetie, how was your flight? Did you find her?" It was the ironic voice of Michael's ex-wife.

"What do you want?" he answered. "It's two o'clock in the morning in New York. Are you drunk again?"

"No. As a matter of fact, I was drunk for sixteen years living next to a man who never really loved me, but now I am completely sober. So, did you find her?"

"Listen, I am on a business trip and I don't have time for this nonsense. I know you must have told Jeremiah that you have some type of emergency, so he gave you my hotel number, but this is not a joke to me. I am busy," Michael said.

"Come on, sweetie. You know I know you. We've been divorced for seven years, but you are still the same. I called your home this morning and your friend, or whoever that was, told me you are on a business trip to Portugal. You are hardly surviving with your book publishing and now you suddenly have money to travel to Portugal. So, what kind of business could you have there? It is about her. Isn't it? It's about your obsession."

"Listen, I'm going to hang up now," Michael was getting really nervous listening to her badgering.

"Oh, go ahead. That is what you always do. It is so you. Wouldn't surprise me. Just make sure you don't hang up on her one day when you find her. She must be human after all. And nobody likes to be hung up on. So, be careful."

"Just tell me what you want," Michael demanded.

"Nothing. Just wondering when you're going to stop with this madness. I really don't care. I am happy. I have been over you for a long time already. I'm only thinking about our kids. You don't call them anyway, but they don't need that embarrassment once everybody realizes how crazy you are. When are you going to get back to reality? Instead of spending money on a plane tickets, you could get a good psychiatrist. Why can't you, like all crazy people, go to psychiatrist and share your nightmares and then act like a normal person. Is that so hard?"

"Listen, please try to understand. I really had a long flight. I am tired. I have an important meeting today. Can't you just forget me for a day? What's your problem? Did your boyfriend ditch you and you are putting that back on me?"

"No, you listen. My boyfriend didn't ditch me. As a matter of fact, he just proposed a few weeks ago and I accepted. I am perfectly happy. I can't wait to get rid of your last name. After all, it was always reserved for her. Wasn't it? I never saw anybody as sad as you when we finally registered in the county clerk office after so many years together. But you, Michael, need to get some help. I don't care if you ruin your life. I don't care about you. But you will ruin our children as well. They are grownups and they still don't understand what happened to you. Get back to reality. When you told me about your dream that day on Brighton Beach, just before we got a divorce, I thought it was a mid-life crisis. A man needing to prove his manhood by running after young women. But then I realized it wasn't that. If you wanted younger women, New York was full of easy women. They would all be happy to please a man like you. It was something worse. It was an obsession. You were chasing your dreams. It is still an obsession and you need to get out of it. For your own good. You should accept that you are sick and that you need help."

Michael hung up the phone and turned to other side. He really didn't need this wake up call. 'She must be drunk again,' he thought.

Chapter Ten
The Lost Life

"Finally, he came to the point in life when he started believing whatever it was that he was missing must have not been of this world."

Michael couldn't sleep anymore. The phone call from his ex-wife really annoyed him. She always knew how to disturb him and trigger depressive thoughts. He started thinking about his life. Pictures from the past were flashing in his mind. He really messed it up. All of those years passed by with so many opportunities. Sometimes he thought that he had really wasted his life. In spite of many obvious achievements, he felt like a loser.

It was quite different up to a few years ago when he believed that he was a true renaissance man. He wasn't the only one thinking that. Many people around him perceived him to be that way. And indeed, he was a man of many talents. But, even though he was successful in many different fields, he never quite completed any of his endeavors. Whenever he would reach a point on any path that would guarantee safe and prosperous future growth, he would lose interest in it. It wasn't challenging enough anymore. And he would turn to completely different things.

Right out of college, he worked as a journalist and photo reporter for several major newspapers in his hometown. Everybody thought he would make it big in journalism, but he decided it wasn't what he wanted.

One day, he surprised all of his friends with a decision to apply for a job position of a security guard. At the time, he already had a Degree in Journalism. It looked odd that he would go after a low paying and, in his case, meaningless career. Of course, he didn't care much about the opinions of others, so he became an armed guard in the bank. Only after a year at the job, he was promoted to Chief of Security. It was a responsible managerial position and it seemed like he was heading somewhere in his life. But again, he wasn't happy and one day, without explanation, he left.

Then, after a while, he started working in a bakery, learned a trade, and three years later he was already a pastry chef in the famed Waldorf Astoria Hotel in New York. The restaurant reviewers were predicting a great future in the culinary arts for him and his name was appearing in the food section of the New York Times with accolades for his creations. It seemed that Michael had found his calling again. It was a profession where he was able to express his creative side and the pastries he was making were real pieces of art. Again, he didn't like it. Something was missing, so he left.

Then he opened up his own bakery and it was an instant success. Soon he opened up two more. People around him were already talking about the chain of bakeries that he would have in the future. One day, he just walked into the office of his business partner, threw his keys on his partner's desk and said, "I am not happy, I am leaving." Then, he left.

Next, he had a catering company working for New York's rich and famous. The list of his clients was from the "Who's Who" in New York. Needless to say, he got bored with that too.

His private life wasn't any better. Married three times, he would always break up relationships with almost no reason. He just wasn't happy. Something was always missing, but he just didn't know what.

Finally, he came to the point in life when he started believing whatever it was that he was missing must have not been of this world. Otherwise, he would have found it already. He decided to start an inner search for what he truly wanted. He wanted to understand himself in order to find peace and happiness. Like in everything else, he was successful in this field too. He joined Brotherhood of Freemasons in New York and became a well-known and respected esoteric researcher, antique book collector, lecturer, writer, and publisher. People were quoting his thoughts and some were seeing a spiritual teacher in him. Alas, he was lecturing about matters of our inner beings and souls, but he still couldn't find his soul. He was unhappier than ever before. Disappointed with himself and everything around him, he pulled back from his active social life, even avoiding his closest friends and family.

Then one night he had a dream. In his dream an angel told him, that he should go and search for a thirty-three years old woman that carries in her the biggest secret of human kind—the Holy Grail. The angel told him that when he finds her, he should stay with her and help her deliver the glory of the sacred knowledge to the world. He was also told that he would recognize her because his soul, which he was searching for all his life, was locked in her body. He would finally be able to unite with his soul and feel the completion and the purpose of his existence.

Michael didn't know what to think about his unusual dream and he didn't have much to go on, so he continued with his secluded life and started liking his solitude and peace. He wasn't happy but he was tired of constant changes in his life. At least he had some stability, working as he liked and was able to live with his dreams and thoughts without affecting anybody around. A few years passed.

He moved from New York to Romania, the place of his birth. Even though, his parents died early in Michael's life, he still had some family there and spoke the language. He started a publishing company and for the very first time in his life, he experienced failure. It was a complete disaster. He lost all of his money and left many investors in his enterprise, some of them his longtime friends, very unhappy and angry.

Soon after, he came back to New York with two hundred and thirty dollars in his pocket and no place to stay. All of the people that he left behind throughout his life didn't want him in their lives anymore. He didn't have anybody to turn to for help. He ended up in the Bowery Mission, a shelter for homeless people where he spent almost a year. There, he regained some of his strength and started working as a content writer for several websites and blogs. He also wrote and published a book on alchemy. It seemed that he would be able to come back to himself.

His work paid off. He rented a small apartment in Brooklyn. He wasn't making much money and it wasn't in a form of a steady weekly or monthly income, but he was able to maintain his living with his writing and publishing. Everything seemed to be in order.

One day, while he was online, browsing through Goodreads book social network looking for interesting stuff, he came across the page of a young woman. Her name was Maria. She was Portuguese. The very first thing he noticed was the list of books she posted as her favorite. All of the books, and exactly in the same order, were his favorite as well. 'What a coincidence,' he thought. He was intrigued, so he sent her a friendship request. Maria accepted it. They started exchanging messages about books and writing. She wrote poetry. After only two weeks, he felt some inexplicable closeness with this woman who was at that moment a complete stranger. He didn't know what exactly drew him to her, but he kept communicating.

With every passing day, their conversations were becoming more and more personal. As they were talking online, they realized that both of them had similar issues with their everyday realities. They both felt like they didn't belong to this world, like they were misplaced. They both dreamed about a different life that was more fulfilling than the one they lived. Maria told him about her dream. Yes, she had one too. He didn't know details of her dream, but he started thinking that maybe this woman was the one he was supposed to find. She was the right age as well. She was thirty-three. More he was thinking about that he was more convinced.

Two months of online communication passed very fast. Maria and Michael were spending hours every day till late in the night, sometimes till five in the morning chatting online. At first, they were using g-mail chat but then they switched to Skype video call. It was completely crazy. One day, they spent sixteen hours online without brake. It seemed like they were mesmerized with each other. Like nothing else in the world exist except two of them and their conversations. And it seemed like they have so much to talk about.

Chapter Eleven
Maria

"…all her life she was dreaming of the man that she could never find, and he only existed in her dreams."

More and more every day, Maria was expressing her longing for Michael's presence and her desire for a physical contact. Often she would send selfies of her naked body and initiate erotic conversations. They were driving Michael crazy, but he enjoyed in them too. He never before in his life had such experience. Sometimes, he would ask himself if all of that was real or just a virtual game of the young woman with an old and crazy man.

Michael was completely smitten with Maria's appearance. She was exactly like the woman from his dream. With light brown curly hair, gray eyes, and pale face, she was small, not more than 160cm tall, but with proportional body and sexy curves.

"You are beautiful, Maria!" He would often say.

"No, I am not. I am simple. Just average. And you are blind and in love."

"No, I am not. I know very well what I am talking about. I am quite objective. You are beautiful!" He would repeat.

Maria would just smile and say again: "No, I am not."

The same conversation would take place several times a day, every day. They would never get tired of it.

Maria was teacher of English in the Middle school in Portimao, town in the district of Faro, in the Algarve region of southern Portugal. For last ten years, since graduating from the University of Lisbon, she was working for the Portuguese Department of Education as English teacher with the annual contracts. Almost every year in different school and different place anywhere in Portugal. For some people that would be a burden, but Maria liked moving every year from town to town, from village to village, always meeting new people and making new friends. She enjoyed her solitary life and didn't like long-term commitments. So this style of living was just what she wanted.

In many ways like Michael, she lived in her world of dreams. She was reading a lot, writing poetry, daydreaming, taking long walks, talking to animals and plants, and it that world there wasn't much space for anybody else. She was telling Michael that all her life she was dreaming of the man that she could never find, and he only existed in her dreams. She never believed that she would find this man in the real life, so she decided to stay with him forever in her dreams and never commit to any relationship with another man in the real life. Then Michael showed up and she started thinking that maybe he was the man she was dreaming about. She wasn't sure yet, but she never felt about any man the same way.

It was almost unbelievable how her story was so strikingly similar to his story. 'What was the chance that this was only the coincidence?' Michael thought. He didn't believe in coincidences. He really believed that he was the man she was longing for and that she was the woman he was supposed to find.

Maria was writing poetry in Portuguese and once in a while she would translate her poems, so Michael could read them. Michael loved to read her poetry. Of course, he was in love, and everybody would say that he wasn't objective, but he thought that he never read something so striking like her poetry.

"Maria, you don't realize how good these poems are. You should publish them and have the whole world enjoy in them. These are the words of an angel. You are not a poet. You are an angel."

"Oh, Michael. You don't know what are you saying. You are not objective. These are just scribbles I do for myself and now for you. Sometimes I share with one or two friends online and that's it. I don't want to share this with anybody. Do you know that my parents still don't know that I am writing poetry and I started when I was sixteen?"

"Why they don't know? Why don't you tell them?"

"They wouldn't understand. They are serious people. For them writing a poetry is a silly thing people do. I don't want them to think that I am silly. They already think I am strange because with thirty-three I am still not married. Whenever I go back home for a summer break they bring some local guys to introduce me to. Like having a husband is the only thing I am looking for, ha. And I have to go through this every summer. So, imagine if on the top of that, they find out that I am writing a poetry."

"So what if they find out? They should be happy. I think you should translate your best poems in English and I would publish them for you as a bilingual edition here in New York. I could do the cover and formatting of the book as well."

"Michael, you are crazy!"

"No, I am serious. I think that is something we should start working on right away. And don't say no, because I will not accept no as an answer."

Maria was actually impressed with idea that Michael wanted to publish her poetry. She never before published any of her writings. Few of her friends, who read some of it, told her already before that she should consider publishing, but she was always too shy to offer her work to any magazine or publisher. And now Michael showed up with his crazy idea. So, after few days of negging she accepted Michael's offer and they started working on her book of poetry.

The plan was that in three months, by Michael's birthday in March, they would already have enough translated poems to put book together. Michael was thrilled that they are working on this project together. He was thinking that a published book could be a great opportunity for him to go to Portugal and bring some copies to Maria.

"When book is done, I will sit on the plane, and bring you personally your author's copies."

"Are you serious Michael? You would come all away to Portugal?"

"Yes! I will come! I already decided."

"That is in three months Michael. It will pass fast."

"I know."

"And where will you stay? You can't stay at my place. I live really near the school and I don't think that woman I rent room from would approve off me having guests. Specially not male. That would be really embarrassing?"

"There must be a hotel in Portimao."

"Of course. But Portimao is a small place. Maybe it would be better if you stay in Faro. It's bigger and there are more things to see there."

"I am not coming to see things, Maria. I want to come to be with you."

"I know. But I have to work, Michael. I can't just take time off. Doesn't work like that. I could be with you on weekend and maybe take Monday off if I ask colleague to do classes for me. How long you would stay, anyway?"

"Forever."

"Michael, be serious. How many days would you stay?"

"I don't know. All depends… Maybe a week or so."

"So if you come for a whole week we could have two weekends together. One could be a long weekend if I take Monday off and second weekend just from Friday afternoon till Sunday. Would that work for you?"

"Yes. That would be great. I will start researching Faro online to see where I could stay."

It was the last week in December when Michael and Maria started counting down days until their first meeting in March. The prospect of finally meeting each other made erotic insinuations in their conversations even more intensive. The main subject of conversations was what were they going to do to each other when they meet.

The time difference between New York and Portugal was five hours. They would get online together as soon as Maria would return from work, around six o'clock in the afternoon, which was around one pm in New York. Then they would stay together till late night on Skype, sometimes till five in the morning Portuguese time. They just didn't want to leave each other. They were eating in front of computer screens at the same time; They were doing other work on computer while their Skype was still on. They just didn't want to quit. Sometimes, when it would get very late, Michael would ask Maria to get offline and go to sleep because she had to be at work at eight in the morning. He worried that she would be too tired next day. But she would always refuse, claiming that all she wanted was to be with him.

At the beginning of January, it was just a week in Michael's and Maria's countdown.

"Seventy more days Michael!"

"Did you count the day of my arrival?

"No."

"Then it is sixty-nine." Michael corrected her.

"Oh Michael, this goes so slow..."

"Yes." Michael answered, "I think the same. On the second thought, why we have to wait till March. I can come earlier?"

"But you said March because you wanted to bring to me finished books."

"Yes, I can still come in March. But how if I come earlier just to see you?"

"Michael! Don't joke with me. You want me to have a heart attack?"

"No Maria. I am serious. I was thinking about that this morning. There is nothing that is holding me from coming to you earlier. If I stay like this, in front of computer, looking at you for next sixty- nine days, I will go completely crazy. If I want, I could come tomorrow. All my work is online. Doing it from Faro or from here, doesn't make a bit of difference as long as I have internet. So what do you say?" Michael asked.

"Michael, tell me you are not joking, please."

"No Maria, I am serious. What do you think?"

"If you can do, that would be great. But wouldn't be too expensive to come before March and in a March again? When would you come?"

"I don't know. I would have to look for a good flight. But it is already out of season so tickets must be cheap. I will check and let you know."

"Oh, Michael, that would be great. I can't believe that we will finally be together. I dream every night about you being next to me…our bodies touching…I can't wait.

Michael had found available plane ticket for next Wednesday, which was in two days. He would be in Lisbon on Thursday morning, take train to Faro and be there in the early afternoon. Maria said that she would come to Faro on Friday evening, right after her work, and stay with Michael till Monday. They were both very excited about their plans.

Michael did research on Faro. He was surprised to learn that the cost of living in Portugal is much lower than in New York. According to his calculations, for fifty percent of the minimum monthly income in the US, one could live quite decent in Portugal. Hotel prices were lower as well. Michael discovered that the oldest still operating hotel in Faro was called Santa Maria. And the room in the hotel for one night was only thirty-nine dollars. 'It would be good and appropriate to stay there with Maria,' Michael thought. He went on the hotel website and booked a room for two for a week.

When Maria finally got offline and went to sleep, Michael stayed in front of the computer still for some time thinking about what he just did. It was bold and crazy move to decide to go to Portugal so fast. Of course, Michael wouldn't be Michael if he wouldn't come up with bold and crazy ideas. He decided to travel to Portugal in order to be close to the woman he loved. This happened in less than three months after they had started communicating. But for Michael, there was nothing unusual in it. Doing things fast, without much preparation, was the story of his life. Somehow, he was sure that Maria was the one he was supposed to find. For him, it was the explanation of all the restlessness and unhappiness he felt with anything and anybody throughout his life. He felt that destiny brought him to the point where he should be united with this woman. And everything that she was telling him was fitting so perfectly in his line of thoughts. 'What were the odds that both of them feeling the same if it was not true?' Michael thought, 'It must be true.'

Chapter Twelve
The Evening Train From Portimao

That Friday evening
As the lights turned on
She walked out of the train car
And left on the pavement
Her footprints
Like music notes
From Moonlight Sonata
Since then I carry on my lips
A kiss as glorious as Milky Way
And I am looking for a word
That will describe her magic
I was born that evening
On the Faro train station
An orphan with no past
Deceived by the future
Accused by my own words
Cursed to love
Without ceasing
Enchanted goddess of longing

Michael was standing on the platform of the Faro train station waiting for the train from Portimao arriving at 9:04 p.m. She was on that train. Finally, they would meet.

It was an unusually warm January night, even for Faro. Michael just arrived from New York the day before. For almost three months he was dreaming about the moment he would meet Maria and there he was on the station platform just a few minutes away from seeing her. The train arrived. People were getting off and then Michael saw her.

His heart was pounding. She was tiny. Hardly five-foot tall, but very proportional. She was the most beautiful woman he had ever seen. He found her curly brown hair, pale skin, her spectacular light blue almost gray eyes, her lips, her nose, her cheeks, her body, her small feet, and her gracious walk so attractive. She was thirty-three years old, but with her baby face, she appeared like she was just twenty. Michael didn't know what to say. He just stared at her.

She stopped in front of Michael and said, "Hello," with such a cute Portuguese accent.

Michael hugged her softly. She smiled.

"How's your trip?" he asked.

"It was good, only hour and a half. I was reading on the train so it went fast."

Michael took the bag she was carrying and they started walking toward the cab outside the station. As they were walking, they kept looking at each other, almost like they were examining each other.

"I was right," Michael said. "You are beautiful. So you can't tell me anymore when I say that you are beautiful, that it is only the picture. I see you now in person. And you are beautiful!"

"You are just in love. I am normal, nothing special," she answered and smiled again.

"No, you are beautiful!"

In the cab going towards the hotel, they kept looking at each other. There was a sense of excitement between them that both of them could feel.

Upon arriving in the hotel room, she unpacked her bag, looked around the room, commented on the hotel, and then she stopped in front of Michael.

"At last, we are together. I told you I would come to Portugal and I am here," he said and put his hands through her hair, softly touching her long neck. Her skin was very white and baby soft.

"You know, I am very shy," she said.

"Yes, I know. We will go slowly. You are so precious my love. Don't worry."

They went out to a nearby restaurant to have a dinner. They had a pleasant time. They were talking about the countless hours they spent in front of the computer chatting to each other till late into the night. They were talking about their dreams, the strange way they fell in love with each other online, over long distance. In previous months they exchanged so many thoughts and they felt like they had known each other forever. Finally, Maria took Michael's hand, looked straight into his eyes and said, "I love you Michael."

He was the happiest man in the world that night. Michael heard the same words so many times from her online, on Skype, but now it was different. She was there, sitting across from him, holding his hand. They were together. All Michael was thinking was that his dream had come true. That was the woman he was supposed to find.

They were walking back to the hotel. She looked so beautiful under the yellowish street lights. He loved the way she moved, smiled, and spoke. Her voice was angelic, but it wasn't only about the way she looked. He adored everything about her. It was what was inside her, everything from her mind and reasoning to her sense of humor. I would do anything, just to see that smile and hear that voice forever, Michael thought. He knew he would never want anyone else for as long as he lived. She is the one. There is no one else.

For Michael falling in love with that woman was very real and deep. He didn't remember ever experiencing anything like that. Everything before seemed so superficial, so fake, like he never loved anybody before. Then, they met online, and finally in person, and everything changed. For many years he thought of himself to be a cold, lying, and unfaithful skirt chaser that could never commit in relationships, but at that moment he felt like he had found his destiny. It seemed like she was the woman he wanted all his life.

The answer to everything Michael loved and admired in women was right there in her dreamy eyes and her mystic smile. There was a particular pride in that smile and nobleness in her facial lines and in the set of her small nose. As they were walking, he wanted to hold her hand, but she pulled her hand back. "I am sorry, but I don't like to show my feelings in public. I don't like holding hands or kissing in public," she said.

He then placed his arm softly on her shoulder. She didn't mind that. They arrived at the hotel and walked up to the room. As they entered, without words, she turned towards Michael, pressed her body to his and they kissed. The kiss was long, deep, and passionate with tongues fiercely invading their senses. They almost could not breathe anymore, but didn't want to break the kiss. Their hands were fervently stroking over each other's body. They slowly undressed each other, throwing clothing to the side. Once naked, they laid on the bed and kept kissing.

Michael continued gently touching her body. He felt desire racing through his body. He then placed his hands over Maria's breasts, massaging them tenderly. With his fingers he traced soft circles around her nipples, tweaking them, gently at first, then harder, then lowering his head and delicately licking and sucking them. He could hear her heart beating fast and her excited moans. Her skin was pale and smooth. He enjoyed the pleasant and discreet scent of her perfume.

He placed his left hand under her tiny but long neck, taking it in a strong grip. He kissed her neck and gave her a gentle love bite. She trembled in excitement. Their lips met again in a passionate kiss with their tongues rousing as wild animals caught in a deep cave. He moved his right hand between her legs. Her pussy was wet and hot and he began to rub her clitoris with his fingers. Maria moved her hand between their bodies and took a hold of his erect penis. She spread her legs and gently pulled his penis towards her pussy. "Get in, I want to feel you," she said. Michael pressed the head of his penis on the opening of her wet pussy. He moved slowly at first, forward and back a few times until his penis was lubricated with the warm juices from her vagina and then in a quick move he slid deep into her. They both sighed in excitement. He pushed even harder as their bodies were rhythmically moving faster and faster towards ecstasy. "Yes, yes my baby," Michael rumbled while exhaling. He grasped her buttocks with his right hand sticking his middle finger into her anus.

She was clutching his back with her arms and pressing her fingers into his skin while kissing his neck and shoulders. Then suddenly, she moved her head back and opened her mouth with a passionate moan. She came. As she was gasping for air, her body started trembling and she moaned again. She came again. Michael came at the same time. He pressed his penis deep into her vagina as he was ejaculating. As he was filling her with his sperm he said victoriously, "Yes, baby, yes." Ejaculating into Maria's vagina was very important for Michael. It was like claiming possession, like leaving a mark, like a completion of the unity.

He was laying on top of Maria. His penis was still inside of her but they were not moving. Just breathing. Enjoying the aftermath of ecstasy. Enjoying the unity of their bodies.

"I love you, Maria. I adore you."

"I love you too, Michael."

For both of them this was a desired completion of the feelings they were sharing online for months, day after day, chat after chat. They were talking and dreaming about this physical encounter for so long. Finally, it happened. They consummated their love. Their bodies merged. Their souls united into one in absolute completion.

He moved beside her and started stroking her hair softly with his hand.

"So, did you like it?"

"Yes," she said quietly and smiled. "Very much. But you came inside me, didn't you?"

Michael didn't answer. He just smiled with an innocent expression on his face.

"I told you that I don't use any protection and I don't want to be pregnant. I am not ready for that. You have to be careful. If I get pregnant, you will never see me again."

"Don't worry, it will not happen. Men of my age don't have a sufficient number of spermatozoids to impregnate a woman. It is very unlikely. It will not happen."

He was lying. That was really stupid comment he made. He knew that she could get pregnant, but he didn't mind. As a matter of fact, he was hopping she would. He wanted to have a son with her. It was a crazy thought. He already had four daughters from previous marriages. They were all adults now. His youngest daughter was already twenty-two. In his position and with his age, the last thing that one would want was yet another child, but somehow, Michael felt that his child with Maria would be a very special child. He didn't know why, but from the very beginning of meeting Maria online, the thought of having a son with her became for him almost an obsession. After all, he wanted to spend the rest of his life with Maria, and it was part of his dream. Just as Archangel had told him.

Passionate and full of desire for each other, they were making love all night. Finally, in the morning, she fell asleep with her head resting on his chest. He looked at her face for a while thinking how happy he was. It was a dream come true. He hoped it would never stop. Then he fell asleep too.

Chapter Thirteen
The First Weekend

"Michael would occasionally joke that the two of them were really just two opposite aspects of the very same person like one soul divided between two bodies of male and female."

When they woke up, it was already one in the afternoon. They decided to go out, eat something and explore Faro. Maria lived for the last six months in Portimao, but she had never been in Faro before.

Faro is a southernmost city in Portugal. It is the capital of the Algarve region with its origins as a habitat dating back to prehistory. Medieval fortress with an old town within its walls, Faro cathedral from the thirteenth century, many old buildings dating back to medieval times, a marina, beautiful sandy beaches, Ria Formosa lagoon, charming taverns serving local specialties, mild and stable Mediterranean clime, warm people—it all makes Faro a very attractive destination for tourists from all over the world. The tourism and hospitality industry are the main source of income for most of its inhabitants.

Michael and Maria walked out of the hotel and turned left onto Rua de Martinha. It was a street closed for traffic, with the pavement made out of traditional Portuguese tiles, and with cafes, stores, and restaurants lined up on both sides of the street. All of the cafes had outdoor seating areas.

It was a sunny Saturday afternoon with temperature in the sixties and they decided to start their day with coffee in an outdoor café.

"In Portugal you start your day with espresso coffee and pastel de nata," Maria said.   "Pastel de nata is a Portuguese egg tart pastry."

Michael liked pastel de nata. It was a nice vanilla flavored custard inside a flaky pastry shell. He also liked the fact that he could smoke in the outdoor café, something that he couldn't do anymore in New York. Just after two days, he was already impressed with Faro. The pace of life was so much slower than in New York and people seemed warm and friendly. Almost everybody he met spoke a bit of English.

"I love this weather!" Michael said.   "Do you know that there was two feet of snow and temperatures below zero when I left New York on Thursday."

"Ha, ha, what a difference! So, do you like it here?" Maria asked.

"Of course, I do. But the best part is that you are here. That is why I want to move here."

"You are really crazy Michael. Are you sure about that? It's a big step. And I can only come to be with you on weekends and still, not even all weekends. I told you already that I enjoy my solitude and sometimes I like to spend weekends alone."

"I know that Maria. I don't want to pressure you into spending time with me when you don't feel like it, but I need to be close to you."

"And what about if I move to another part of Portugal at the end of this year. You know that The Ministry of Education is sending me to a different school every year. I never know before August where I will be living next school year. What will you do then?"

"I will move too. I don't mind."

"But how will you live? Do you have enough money? You need to have some backup money too. You don't know Portuguese. What about your work in New York? How will you do that? Can you do it from here?"

"I did my research already Maria. Life here is much cheaper than in New York. Only with the amount of money that I pay for rent back in New York, here I can pay rent, utilities and all monthly expenses. I think I will be able to cover living costs here. When it comes to my work I can do it from anywhere, as long as I have internet. I do everything online anyway."

Everything wasn't that simple. The truth was that Michael's savings could enable him to come to Faro one more time, rent an apartment, and have for two months of living at the most. And that would be it. If he doesn't make more money working from Faro, he would be in a big problem. He didn't worry about that part as much. Often in his life, he had been in financially risky situations and he was always able to find a way out. All that was important to him at that moment was to be close to Maria. Nothing else really mattered.

"So, what do you say? Should I start looking for an apartment today?"

"You realize that everything is not that simple, do you? You are tourist and can stay without visa only six months. After that, you would have to apply for a resident status or different kind of visa. I don't know how it works, but you would have to take care of all of that."

"Of course. I can do all of that when I come next time." Michael answered.

"Okay then. I think you are really crazy. I guess, that's why I love you. We can look today and tomorrow for an apartment. I will help you with that," Maria said and smiled.

They had their lunch in the same café and then spent the afternoon walking around the old fortress and Faro marina. They enjoyed their time together. Michael was almost twenty-three years older than Maria, but in spite of the age difference they had so many things in common. Their characters, habits, and interests seemed to be so similar. Michael would occasionally joke that the two of them were really just two opposite aspects of the very same person like one soul divided between two bodies of male and female. All occasional differences were only coming out from their specific gender and age characteristics.

Maria was born in Northern Portugal. Her father had a vineyard in Douro region, and she grew up surrounded with the beauties of the countryside on the hills overlooking Douro River. She loved walking over the meadows and through the valleys and forests. Living in the secluded stone house surrounded with vineyards, she didn't have many friends as a child or a school playground nearby. Pastures and woods became her playground and small forest animals became her best friends. She became devoted to nature and it was a source of her energy and inspiration. She would spend all of her holidays and vacations back in her parents' home. She never thought of going anywhere else. Once she told Michael that she could see herself in the future, at an old age, living in the same house she grew up in. That was the place she felt happiest

The other reason she would go to her parents' home whenever she could, was her strong attachment to her family. Her parents were simple, but hard working people and they raised Maria to be a person with a strong sense of family, responsibility and duty. She started working right out of the school and never quit or changed her job.

From what she told Michael, it seemed that her father was strict, and remained a strong presence in Maria's life. Early on, she learned to keep her feelings to herself, afraid of her father's disapproval or criticism. Her parents knew little about her private life. She wrote poetry since she was a teenage girl and her parents never knew that. Michael was preparing to publish her first collection of poems and she already told Michael that she didn't want her parents to find out about it.

Almost every year she would be transferred to another school, to another town. She would make new friends, start relationships, and then have to do the same thing again next year. She learned to live in solitude and enjoy it. She was afraid of commitments knowing that her way of life would clash with any possible commitment.

Besides her family, the only other permanent part of her life was with her friends online. She could be with them at anytime, anywhere she was. She could talk to them about anything. It was her own virtual world and her parents could not interfere or comment on it, but she had dreams too. And her dreams included a man—a man that she created in her dreams and thought that she would never find in the real world. Then, suddenly, Michael showed up claiming to be that man.

"You know, Michael, it will take time for me to get used to the idea that you are here. I am a bit afraid. It's a big change for me and especially for you and I don't want to feel responsible if this doesn't work for you."

"It will work," Michael said. "It will work because I am not asking anything from you. I am not making any conditions. I simply feel that I need to be close to you. That is all."

They went back to the hotel and looked online for available apartments for rent in Faro. There were many. They decided to keep looking for text two months, and when Michael get back in March, make appointments to go see those he likes. Then they went to dinner at a nearby tavern.

They had a pleasant time with good food and good wine, chatting about her poetry, work, family, and Michael's plans for the future. The waiter serving them looked at them with curiosity. He saw that she was Portuguese and that Michael was a foreigner. The age difference was obvious. Michael and Maria were jokingly guessing what his thoughts about them might be.

Back at the hotel, they started kissing while still in the elevator going to their room. They made love all night again, but now even with more passion than the first night. Full of desire and already accustomed to each other's body, they surrendered to the pleasures of their love. She asked him to be careful and not ejaculate in her. He said he would be, but of course, he wasn't. He finished inside of her again. And again. He wanted so badly to have a son with her.

On Monday night Maria went back to Portimao. The first week in Faro passed fast for Michael. During the day, while Maria was working, he would roam through the old town in Faro, enjoy pastries in the garden of the small café near hotel and watch people passing by. "Portuguese women are really good looking," he thought. "There is something so captivating about them. Some magic. Something beyond physical beauty. And I have the most beautiful of them all." He smiled on these thoughts.

Evenings he would spend in the hotel room talking on Skype to Maria till late night. For them, this was already standard practice. Except, this time, they were much closer. Sometimes, he would joke that he would sit on the train for Portimao and come knocking on her doors.

Next Friday evening, Maria was back in Faro. They spent weekend together again. But this time, they almost didn't come out of the hotel room except for the occasional fast meals. Maria was insisting on paying half of all expenses they made.

"No way Maria! I invited you to eat out. I am paying for this." Michael said.

"If you don't let me pay half I will not go out with you ever again. You need to save money if you are going to move here and not to spend on me."

Michael wouldn't let her pay anything, but he liked her attitude.

On Monday morning they got up early in the morning. They went to the Faro train station. Maria took the first train back to Portimao to be there on time for work and Michael took train to Lisbon an hour later. His flight to New York was at two o'clock that afternoon.

Chapter Fourteen
The Promise

"Your love is so pure, so deep, so universal, expressed to the whole of the creation, that directing your love to one single person often seemed to you like a limitation of your feelings, like the loss of the freedom to be who you really are."

After just a couple of hours of sleep they got up at ten in the morning. They took a shower together, enjoying rubbing each other's body, but they had to rush. Their appointment with the real estate agent was at eleven. They didn't have much time. They had coffee in the hotel and then ran out to the meeting.

The real estate agent was a woman in her forties and she spoke English. She didn't see anything unusual in an American renting an apartment in Faro. There were quite a few Americans already living in Faro. They all appreciated the benefits of the Mediterranean climate, easy pace of life, and a much lower cost of living than in the US.

Michael told her that he was writing a book with the story taking place in Faro and that he wants to be at the location of the events that he is writing about. She thought that was quite interesting. Of course, she didn't fail to ask about Michael and Maria's connection. They told her they were friends working for the same publisher. She just smiled and didn't inquire further.

She showed them four apartments and one of them seemed like a place Michael could enjoy. It was the one-bedroom apartment within walking distance from downtown Faro and the rent was reasonable. The real estate agent called the landlord and he agreed to meet Michael on Monday morning.

It was already two in the afternoon when they finished with the real estate agent. Maria had to catch the train back to Portimao at 5:18 that evening, so they decided first to go eat something, go back to the hotel to pick up Maria's stuff and then go to the train station.

They went to the Adega Nova restaurant, just a few blocks from the hotel. The Adega Nova was built in an old tile and brick warehouse, yet had the look of a traditional Portuguese bodega. The place was very popular with the local crowd and they served traditional Portuguese dishes. Maria and Michael ordered a cod dish with potatoes and veggies and a bottle of red wine.

"When you left in January, for a while, I was afraid that I'll never see you again. We had two wonderful weekends together. It was like a dream. I wasn't sure if I was dreaming or you were really here. Then talking to you on the Skype for almost two months every day without being able to touch you, to feel you, it was really tough. But now, when you are here again, I am so happy."

"You know; I feel the same. Before I came last time, it was hard not being close to you. But then after I was here in January and left, it was much harder. I missed you every day and every night. Hopefully we wont have that problem any more now that I am here. Now I live in Faro." Michael smiled while saying that. He was excited about the apartment.

"I can't believe we found an apartment the very first day we started looking for it!" he said.

"I think Faro was overdeveloped. There are many vacant apartments for rent and the economy in Portugal is not so good. Even tourism is slowing down," Maria answered. Then she said: "And I still can't believe you gave up your apartment in New York just like that. What did you tell your friends?"

"That I am moving to Portugal."

"And? How did they react?"

"They were surprised. But that's really not important." Michael said.

"What if doesn't work for you here? What are you going to do then?" Maria asked.

"That option doesn't exist for me. I know it will work. Don't you see that everything falls in its place just as it should. We found the apartment. And I will make it look beautiful for my baby and me."

The apartment was furnished, but it still needed a few things. They spent time discussing what he needed for the apartment and where he could get it. Maria told him she would make a few things for his apartment. She liked to crochet and she was going to make placemats for the dining room and a rug for the bathroom.

"You know," Maria started, "next weekend I will have to go north to my parents' house. I haven't been back home in a while, but the following weekend I will be back here again. That will give you some time to settle into your new place, learn more about Faro and maybe make some new friends. You have to start learning Portuguese. Many people in Portugal speak English, especially here, being a tourist area, but if you want to live here you have to know language. It will be easier."

"And of course," she continued, "while I am in my parents' home, we can talk in the evenings online. So, make sure that the first thing you do when you move into the apartment is to go to the Vodafone store or some other internet provider and get a router for the internet. It takes usually two to three days for them to come and install."

"Yes, that is most important," Michael said. "Having the internet for me is essential. I can't work without it. All of my work I do online."

After they finished dinner and discussing about the apartment, they were just sitting quietly, sipping their wine, holding hands over the table and looking at each other. It was again an exciting weekend for both of them. It was beginning of March. For a moment Michael had a flashback about the beginning of March two years before, when he arrived to New York from Bucharest. It was something he wanted to forget. Now he was sitting with a gorgeous young woman having a good time and he didn't want memories like that in his head.

"Did I tell you already that you are beautiful Maria?"

"No, I am not. I am an average person. It's only in your eyes. You are in love and when you are in love, your mind is controlled by your heart. So you see what your heart wants you to see," Maria said and smiled. "But anyway thank you for telling me that I am beautiful. It feels good to hear that. I hope you wont stop telling me."

"The way I see it, our eyes serve two masters, our soul and our mind," Michael started. "Our souls see much further than our mind, so it is not a surprise that we often feel what is ahead of us even before it is registered by our physical ability to perceive it. It is really that our soul sees it before our mind. There is this old expression that everybody knows, which says that the eyes are the windows of the soul. I always thought that to be true. But, somehow, whenever I look at your eyes, Maria, I see my soul, not yours. And I don't know what to think about it. It almost feels like my soul was captured by yours and the only way to reconnect to my own soul is through you. It is a weird feeling."

Maria leaned forward over the table, touched Michael's cheek and lips with her hand and whispered, "I love you, Michael." Then she said,

"All of my life, I've seen you only in dreams. I thought that it would stay like that. I had a few relationships before and each time I thought, this is the man from my dreams, but each time it was a disaster and a disappointment. I always thought that I am not a normal person. That there is something different about me. Something not of this world. So, I decided to be alone and to be with my man only in my dreams. And I love my solitude. I enjoy it. And then you showed up. And I love you, but I still have my doubts. I still have my fears if everything that is happening between us is the story from my dreams. Am I still dreaming? Am I going to wake up one day in my regular life and you won't be there? Like you never really existed. Like you were just my virtual man from the virtual world."

"It is interesting that you mention that. I often think about the way we met. Life is always full of surprises," Michael said. "Almost everybody has at least one unusual story to tell. Meeting somebody in the virtual world of social media and falling in love without ever seeing each other in person doesn't seem to be unusual any more. It can happen to many people, but it was unusual when it happened to me. I was struggling with my feelings. How much of it was real. How much of it was just a dream. Is it possible that all of it was just a play between two lonely people? Was this woman the one I really love or just the product of my imagination and of my desire to love and be loved. Would I be able to make this dream come true or was I heading into disillusionment and tragedy? But now when I met you, Maria, I know that you are real and you are the one I was supposed to find. So, I need to tell you something very important and I want you to remember that forever."

Michael took both of Maria's hands and continued.

"I know that you still have doubts about me and about your love for me. I know that you love your independence and your solitude. I know that you have issues with your parents and that out of fear of their disapproval, you would never go to them and tell them that you are in a relationship with a man who is twenty years older than you and I am not asking that from you. Just love me as you do. Your love is so pure, so deep, so universal, expressed to the whole of creation, that directing your love to one single person often seemed to you like a limitation of your feelings, like the loss of the freedom to be who you really are.   I understand all that. You were longing for the man that will understand and love you the same way you love, without asking from you what you couldn't give. I think I am that man, Maria. I'm not asking you for any commitments, but I promise you my soul, my heart and my body. They will be only yours. I promise you my unconditional love forever. And I am not asking for anything in return. Just allow me to be close to you. I need to be close to you. I will never stop loving you. And if you stop loving me as a man, allow me to stay your friend, your best friend. I will not press you into living with me or marrying me, but if you ever decide that it is what you desire, I will always be here for you waiting, as long as I live."

"But Michael, don't promise me that. I can't yet promise you anything. It is not fair for you."

"No, it is my promise and it will stay. You don't have to promise anything."

After dinner, they picked up Maria's bag from the hotel and they walked to the train station. Maria left her bag on the seat in the train and then walked out to say goodbye to Michael.

"Call me when you arrive home," Michael said. "I will hook up my laptop to the hotel's wifi so we can talk on Skype tonight if you want."

"Yes, I would love that. I will call you at seven tonight, "Maria answered. They hugged and they said, "I love you" to each other and then she went back to the train. She sat next to the window and sent a kiss to Michael. He sent her a kiss back. The train left.

Chapter Fifteen
The New Beginning

"Michael—the man with the key—My King. I love you forever."

On Monday morning Michael woke up early. It was 6:00 a.m. He slept only for two hours after talking to Maria online until four o'clock in the morning. She must be very tired, he thought.

Even though he was excited about the apartment and meeting with the landlord, Michael still worried. He didn't know the procedures of renting in Portugal, but if it was anything like in New York, he would have a problem. His credit was bad, he couldn't provide any references because he was self-employed, and he had money only for the first month of rent and the one-month deposit. His meeting was at nine so he had to get ready.

He put on one of two suits that he had brought with him from New York, a nice shirt and a tie. He wanted to make a good impression as a professional and serious person.

The top floor apartment was located on the Rue Capitáo Jose Veira Branco No. 16, in the center of Faro. It was a large one bedroom, in the well-maintained seven story building, with a living room which included a dining room area, with a spacious kitchen, and a big terrace facing south with a view of the marina and the sea. Michael liked the fact that it was on the seventh floor. It was a number symbolizing god's creation. From the windows in the living room facing north, there was a view of the hills and mountains surrounding Faro.

Michael met the landlord at exactly nine in the apartment. The landlord was an easy-going elderly Portuguese man who didn't speak English, but understood a bit. They managed somehow to communicate with each other. He asked only for the first month's rent and for a deposit. He didn't ask for any references or documents. He showed Michael around, explained to him about electric bills and hot water, gave him keys, took the money and left.

Michael stayed in the apartment. He couldn't believe. It was so easy. He had his apartment in Faro. And he would be able to be with Maria. He was the happiest man in the world. He walked around the apartment looking at bedroom, closets, kitchen cabinets, bathroom, hallway, and terrace. He needed few things like bed sheets, pillows, and towels. But besides those things, toiletries, and food, everything else was there. 'He would be able to manage till the end of the month,' he thought. 'And with some luck he would do a project or two before the end of the month and be able to subsidize his living.'

He went back to the hotel, packed up his luggage, checked out and came back to the apartment. The whole afternoon he spent shopping. By the evening he had everything he needed.

He wanted to celebrate, so he bought a bottle of wine. In the evening, he was standing on the terrace, looking at the city lights and the reflection of the moon on the sea in the distance. The sky above was huge and full of stars. They seemed so close. He was sipping his wine and thinking how lucky he was. His move to Faro turned out to be easy. If it wasn't meant to be that way, if it wasn't the right thing, it would not happen that easy. God was on his side, he thought. The whole universe was with him.

He didn't have internet yet, so he couldn't be online with Maria, but they spent some time talking on the phone. He didn't fall asleep until late. He was excited. He finished the bottle of wine and finally around two in the morning he went to bed. In his own bed in his own apartment.

The next morning, Michael went to the Vodafone store to get the internet. Signing up for the internet was easy and didn't cost him much. They told him that by the end of the week they would come to install the router.

The next two weeks Michael spent settling in the apartment. The Vodafone people came when they said they would, so now he had internet and house phone.

On March 14th was Michael's birthday. It was Friday and Maria came. She made a birthday card for him and wrote on it, "Michael—the man with the key—My King. I love you forever." She gave him her note book with her poems and drawings. He was so happy.

"I will keep this notebook and cherish it all of my life. This is the most valuable thing anybody has ever given me for my birthday."

Following weekend Maria came again. They almost didn't go out. They spent days fixing things in the apartment, cooking, eating, and talking. They spent nights making love.

Before she left on Sunday afternoon, she cooked soup for Michael to have for a few days, cleaned the bathroom and ironed a few of his shirts. Michael didn't ask her to do that, but she wanted to take care of him. He thought that was very sweet. He didn't remember the last time somebody pressed his shirts for him. She also left some of her clothing and toiletries, so she wouldn't have to carry them with her each time she came to visit. Michael liked that too. 'She was getting comfortable, moving in slowly,' he thought. That was what he was hoping for.

Michael's work was going well. He got a big web design project from New York that would give him enough income to live for the next three months. Time was passing by. Michael spent weekdays working. He rearranged the furniture in the living room to look like an office. He liked to feel like being in a work space. On evenings, he would take long walks around Faro, down to the seaport, through the Faro fortress, and back to the center of Faro where he would enjoy evenings in the outdoor cafes having coffee and watching people pass by. People in the local stores and cafes started to recognize him as a regular customer and began greeting him. He befriended a couple of neighbors and the owner of the local book store and once in a while he would have coffee with them.

Maria visited on weekends. On Friday afternoons, Michael would clean out the house, buy food for the weekend and go to the train station to wait for Maria. He prepared dinner on Friday nights and she cooked on Saturdays. For Michael, being with Maria on weekends was like being in a heaven. Everything was so perfect. It seemed that Maria felt the same way. They enjoyed each other's company. They enjoyed making love. They enjoyed talking. Every single moment together felt precious. And it seemed like weekends together were not enough. During the week, they continued with their routine of spending hours on the internet talking until late in the evening.

Michael wanted so much to live with Maria. He knew that in her mind she was not ready yet. She lived for too long by herself and she got used to it. She still feared her parents' disapproval and didn't want to face them with actions that they may not like. Michael knew all of that, but he hoped that her need to be with him would grow as time was passing by and he was willing to wait. He also hoped that she would get pregnant and that something like that would change things, allowing them to go in the direction he wanted. Each time they would make love, he would finish in her. She would always make a comment "Michael, you were not careful again." Michael would just smile and look innocently at her like the boy who just broke the vase and was pretending like it was somebody else.

Chapter Sixteen
Money Troubles

"In my mind Maria, being with you is worth risking everything."

The first three months in Faro passed so quickly for Michael. The weather was great, people around him were friendly, and Maria was with him regularly every weekend. Everything seemed perfect. Michael and Maria were happy.

The beginning of June brought worries. After the web design project, he had just finished, there were no new jobs coming in. Michael called few companies in New York that he was freelancing for, but they just didn't have any new work for him. He was suspecting that the fact that he was in Faro and not in New York caused the lack of new jobs. Most of his clients were Pastors of the Churches affiliated with the Bowery Mission. When he was back in New York, he used to go regularly to his clients' offices, picked up a project, worked from home and sent them back. He wouldn't choose or pick the projects. He would accept everything - book formatting, book covers, editing, web design, copywriting. Once the project was done, he would still go back to the clients to discuss it. In spite of the fact that all of his work was online, he liked that personal touch and it worked for him. It was bringing him more work. He knew how to talk to people, but now he couldn't do that. He was in Faro. Was it possible that distance played a role in not getting more projects? He really depended on his work from New York. He knew that it would be very hard for him to get any work in Portugal. He didn't speak the language and he didn't put enough time into studying it, anyway. He spoke English with Maria, and almost everybody around him spoke some English. On other hand, the economy in Portugal was in crisis and there were not many job opportunities. Besides, he didn't know where he would look for job if he had to. Also, he was still in Portugal on tourist visa, without right to work.

In spite of everything, Michael thought that it was just a temporarily setback and that new jobs would come. He had just paid his June rent and bills and held onto some extra cash to put him through a couple of weeks. Something would come in the meantime, he thought.

Three weeks passed. In a week Michael would have to pay his rent and he even didn't have enough money to buy a pack of cigarettes. Maria came that Friday as usual. Michael waited for her at the train station. On the way home he was quiet. He knew he would have to tell Maria about his financial problems, but he didn't know how. Whatever he would say, he knew it would look bad. He wanted to keep with Maria an image of independent well-to-do man, not a struggling freelancer who was just two years ago in the shelter for homeless people.

"Michael, why are you so quiet? Are you tired? Is it something wrong? "Maria asked while they were walking home from the train station.

"Oh, nothing much. It's my work. It is slowing down. I worry about my income. That's all."

"Maybe it's because of summer. It just began. Usually in summer all businesses get slower. It is normal. Don't worry."

"Yeah. I guess it is summer." Michael said.

"But you are okay with money to put you through the summer, aren't you?" Maria asked.

"Hmm, I am not sure…" Michael said, but than ad fast: "But don't worry, I'll take care of things. It is not the first time."

Maria stopped walking and looked at Michael with the surprise in her eyes. "What do you mean you are not sure? Do you have money for rent and food for next month?"

"Well, not exactly…"

"Not exactly! Michael, you came to Faro three months ago with the idea to live here. You should have had back-up emergency money for at least six months of living, if not for more, and after three months you don't have for a rent. What kind of man would do that?"

"Maria, things don't always work the way we want. But it is not your problem. You don't have to worry. I'll take care of it."

They didn't talk about this subject any more during that weekend. They had a good time and on Sunday night Michael took her to a train station.

Monday morning Michael looked at his pantry and fridge. There was almost no food left. 'He would have to do something,' he thought. He thought of selling his camera. Few months before, he purchased Canon digital camera in New York. It was very useful piece of equipment that Michael was using for his graphic design work. If he managed to sell it, he could make at least two, three hundred Euros. That would help. He walked around Faro looking for stores that buy and sell used electronic equipment. He found two; went there, but they were not interested in buying his camera. That was a blow. Michael was sure that he would be able to sell it.

Following Friday Maria was in Faro again. Only that time Michael didn't have neither any food in the house for over the weekend nor any money. He was flat out broke. On the way home they stopped by a supermarket. Maria bought everything they needed for weekend and some extra food for Michael for next week.

"So what are you going to do about rent?" she asked when they entered apartment.

"Landlord is coming on Monday to pickup rent money. I was thinking to call him before to ask him to wait for a few days, but I'll wait until he comes on Monday and talk to him in person. I think it's better."

"Few days? So you will have some money coming soon?"

"Yes. I think so." Michael answered. He was lying. There was no money coming from anywhere but he didn't want her to know that.

"I still can't understand how you could allow yourself to be in this position. In all my life, I was never late or in default on any of my financial obligation. I hate when people do that. I think it is very irresponsible."

"Maria, sometimes in life there are circumstances that one can't control. Things happen. They can happen to anybody."

"Yes. But you can project things in life. Make plans. Prepare yourself for any potential problems. You moved to Portugal, left everything in New York, and after three months you run out of money. That is not a good planning."

"The only objective I had before coming here was to be with you as soon as possible Maria. Yes, I could plan my moving more carefully, but that would mean staying in New York longer until I accumulate enough savings. I didn't want that. You can't blame me for wanting to be with you."

"I don't blame you Michael. I just want you to live normally and without problems. I am scared that you rushed with all of your decisions and that if things don't work out for you here, I will feel responsible. I don't want to be responsible, Michael."

"No, you don't have to feel responsible. I knew all the risks of coming here and I did it consciously. In my mind Maria, being with you is worth risking everything. So don't blame yourself or me for anything. I am not a kid. I knew what was that I was doing when I set on the plane. And again, I have to tell you: Don't get overwhelmed with this. It is a small problem and I will take care of it. I've been in tight corners before in my life and I always got out. It won't be different now."

"What kind of a tight corners? Maria asked.

Michael didn't answer. He turned his head on the side pretending that he didn't hear her question.

Chapter Seventeen
Shadows From the Past

*"One day you will understand that everything I did in my life
was connected in some way with you."*

"You know, we talk for months every day, all day, but you never told me much about your past. Besides the fact that you were married three times and have three girls, I don't know anything else. Is there anything I should know?"

Michael looked at her. He always wanted to be completely honest with this woman. He was never before completely honest to anybody in his life. But he already starting lying to Maria. He didn't like that. "I should stop with this before it's to late and tell Maria the truth. She deserves that. She is the woman I love,' Michael thought.

"Okay. I think you are right. I haven't told you much about my past. Not because I wanted to hide anything from you, but because I am not very proud of my past. I will tell you. All I am asking you is not to judge me. One day you will understand that everything I did in my life was connected in some way with you."

"With me? Why with me? We found each other six months ago." Maria said with surprise in her voice.

"Yes. But now when I am thinking about my life, from the distance of over fifty years, I can clearly see the pattern and the connections, cause and effect of everything that happened to me. And everything points into one direction: Finding Maria. I finally I have found you. I wish I have found you when I was twenty-five, but it didn't happen then."

"Ha, ha, that was fortunate," Maria said jokingly, "I was five then. You would be accused of pedophilia."

"No, that is not what I meant. I meant I wish that age difference is smaller between us. Anyway, I will tell you everything you should know about your man."

So Michael told Maria everything about his life, including his past business dealings, Bucharest story, failing investments and debt, conflicts that he had with some Freemasons back in New York, and time he spent in Bowery Mission. He thought that the more she knew about his past would help her understand the background of the problems he had. He didn't want her to think that he was a dishonest man or con-man, or a thief. In his mind, he saw himself as a victim of the circumstances that he couldn't handle. Of course, that didn't mean that he was not responsible for his problems. His habit of running away whenever he encountered difficulties in his life, finally caught up with him and he was not able to understand why people that he would leave behind without any explanation were angry and often wanted revenge.

Yet, the more he was telling Maria, the more questions she had. He didn't mind telling her everything. Before Maria, he had never shared anything with anybody. Even when he was married, he never shared with his wives any problems that he would have, but now he felt that he wanted to share everything with Maria. He didn't want to have any secrets. It ended up that what he shared didn't look good.

Maria was concerned. And Michael felt that his life story must be overwhelming for her.

"You should go back to New York Michael, make some money and solve your problems. I love you and I don't want anything bad to happen to you. And you don't have to worry about me. I am here and I will wait for you," she said.

Michael didn't want to take into consideration such an option.

"No, Maria. I will not go back. There is nowhere to go back. Faro is my home now. I gave you a promise that I will be close to you forever. Whatever happens, I will keep my promise. It is a complicated situation, but I will solve it. I always did it before. I will do it now as well."

Michael was concerned as well and very angry with himself. Maria was a straightforward and responsible person. She always took care of all of her obligations, never lived above her means, and never borrowed money from anybody. Michael knew that it would be hard for her to understand all of his circumstances, regardless of how much time he spent explaining it to her. He worried that she would see him as an irresponsible and dishonest man and the worst of it was that Michael knew that in many ways, throughout his life, he was.

Sometimes, he thought of himself as an elephant walking through the china store, breaking everything in his path and still expecting people not to be angry with the damage he made, but rather to admire his strength and his endurance.

The truth of the matter was that Michael was arrogant and selfish. He never had a respect for anything or anybody. Whatever he was doing in his life, he was never truly happy. There was always something that was missing that would make him just leave everything and disappear and he didn't know why. Somehow, he always had a strange feeling that everything he went through had to happen, like it was predestined, like he was paying for his mistakes from some previous life. He didn't think of himself as a bad man. He was an intelligent man with many talents. Everything that he ever did in his life, he did with good intentions. He never thought of hurting, deceiving, or cheating anybody, but somehow, it would always turn out that way. Even the smallest mistakes that he would make would turn into big problems just because he was ignoring them.

Since he had his strange dream, he knew that there must have been a reason for everything that happened to him. He didn't regret anything until he met Maria. Finally, he thought that he had found the purpose of his life. He didn't know exactly what it was, but everything in connection with Maria just seemed right. He became a different man. A man with a soul.

Now he was angry that his past spilled over into their relationship. It was baggage that he didn't want to bring to Maria. He wanted for Maria to feel his pure love and commitment, what he was for her, and not what he had been for other people. The timing of the events cannot be worse, he thought.

Yet, he expected that she would understand. After all, she loved him. They shared unique dreams. Their love for each other was above and beyond any earthly matters. That whole weekend Maria didn't look much happy. Michael knew that she was preoccupied with the thoughts about his past. But he hopped it would pass. Before she left on Sunday night, she gave him forty Euros in cash: "You may need this for cigarettes until your money comes." She said. Michael didn't refuse it.

On Monday, the landlord came to pick up rent. Michael invented a story about some money being stuck in the money transfer from US and asked Landlord to wait a week or two until he solves this issue. Landlord agreed.

The whole week Michael spent trying to come up with the solution. But nothing was coming to his mind. On Thursday, Michael had a morning coffee with his neighbor Francisco. Francisco loved photography and had a real passion for cameras.

"Francisco, would you be interested in buying my Canon. It's sitting around, and I don't use it much, so I'm thinking of selling it? I could give you a good price." Michael said.

"No. Not really. I have three cameras. Thanks. But why are you selling it? Do you need some money?" Francisco asked.

"I am a bit short on cash. Some of my money is stuck in the bank transfer so I am waiting for it."

"How much do you need? Maybe I could help you a bit."

Michael was surprised with this offer from his neighbor.

"I don't know. Maybe four hundred Euros?" Michael said, "To get me through until my money comes."

"No problem Michael. Here it is." Francisco put his hand in his shirt pocket, pulled out a bunch of money, took out eight fifty Euro bills, and handed over to Michael. "I always like to have cash on me. Don't believe much in multibanco machines."

Michael called immediately his landlord to come to pick up rent. With this loan he bought some time to solve his problem. '*God is helping me again. Maybe a new project will come soon,*' he thought.

Chapter Eighteen
Doubts

"In her dream, the man she was in love with was of pure heart and soul, honest, strong, responsible, and without a blemish."

Michael wasn't going to tell Maria about rent until she comes on Friday. And of course, he was not going to tell her that he borrowed money. He was left with fifty Euros for food and he will prepare nice weekend for two of them.

He spent Friday afternoon shopping for food and cleaning the house as usual before her arrival. Then, around five o'clock she called him.

"Michael, I cannot come this weekend. I have some work to do around the house and do my laundry. I have a big pile. But we will be together online anyway. I hope you don't mind."

Michael remembered that Maria told him that she would not be able to come every weekend and not to expect that, but for the last three months, since he came to Faro, she was with him every weekend. Somehow, he felt that her decision not to come had something to do with the problems that he had. He was thinking that maybe he made a mistake by telling her everything, but again, he wanted to be honest with her and not have any secrets. She was the woman that he loved unconditionally and he believed that her love for him was the same.

Michael was right about his assumptions. The following days Maria spent searching online for references to everything that had anything to do with Michael. She was good in Google search and she knew where to look with the information that Michael gave her. Soon, she came across comments that some Masons wrote on various Masonic blogs and websites. Pretty much, they were all similar, referring to Michael as a charlatan and swindler. She knew that everything wasn't so black and white and that there was much more to the whole story, but she didn't like what she found. Even the reviews of Michael's books had bad overtones. It was obvious that they were written by the people who didn't want to write about Michael's book and only wanted to slander him. She found two reviews by the same man about one of Michael's books that were completely opposite. In the first review this man wrote all accolades for the book and the author. In the second review, written a couple years later, he was claiming that Michael didn't know anything about the subject he was writing about. It was obvious that the review was written with the intention to hurt Michael. She didn't know what to think anymore. Suddenly, everything about Michael was so disturbing. Each time, she would find something, she would call Michael to hear his explanation. Each time, he would talk about bad circumstances and destiny without accepting any blame. She just couldn't understand that.

In her dream, the man she was in love with was of pure heart and soul, honest, strong, responsible, and without a blemish. A man who loved everybody and anything around him and Michael seemed to be like that. She could not believe that she made a mistake. But everything about his past was full of lies, deceit, and conflicts with others. He was tainted. Was it possible that he was deceiving her as well? Was this really the Michael that she was spending weekends with and hours on end online?

She always wanted to have a complete life with a sense of purpose, but the one she lived so far, made her feel repulsive and detached. Rejecting uniformity and compromise, she was watching this, for her, a strange phenomenon, of people molding each other in forms suitable for their togetherness. It was the worst kind of degradation and manipulation of one's soul, she thought. It was a twisted picture of warmth and unity like an uncertain experiment in happiness. So, she didn't want any part of this so typical life experience. It was just a spectacle, so distant and unattainable. She didn't know if she would ever be ready for it.

So, for years, she kept running away from her true needs. To her, they were just mindless and frantic echoes of anxiety and adversity. She denied and rejected them like monstrous apparitions, jolting the image of herself. To discard them meant to awaken the spark of desire for change. Constant change. It was the only thing that made her feel herself.

After a long mind quest, she had found peace in being with herself. She learned to enjoy her solitude. Nevertheless, some unclear energy, irrational hallucinations and dreams were accompanying her even when she was completely satisfied. She already felt an intimacy with them and seemed to be seeking the comfort of mind in these dream creations. With them, she was never alone and they were almost always faithfully serving her desires and kept her on the course she was comfortable with. They were sending an unquestionable message to everyone that this was her own world. Or at least, it was like that until she met Michael.

Then, an unexpected multitude of thoughts from Michael spilled over to her. Who was he? What gives him the right to disturb her dreams? His thoughts were like an army of invincible outlaws and the enemies of her common sense. Armed with deception and cunning, artists of fraud and undisputed rulers of manipulation, reinforced with the desire to enter her dreams, and place himself there as the only solution for her destiny. How did he ever managed to get so far?

It seemed like he knew all of her ways. He was almost like the mirror image or the male version of herself. Yet, she wasn't ready to accept him as her counterpart. Her world of dreams was just that—dreams. And he wanted to pull them out and materialize them in time and space. What nerve! What lunacy! He was either a bigger dreamer than herself or a reckless player in the game of life. He made her feel happy and complete, but the idea of achieving that in reality was too scary and too dangerous a thought. She already felt the loss of herself, the collapse of the power of her imagination. She was being suffocated by her own love for this uncommon man.

Even if this conversion of dreams into reality was possible, her everyday life was far too common to fit such glorious dreams, she thought. One or the other would collapse. In some ways, she even liked her life. Of course, it was nothing like her dreams, but it made her feel secure and in control. She never cut the cord with her childhood and that connection with her family was a big portion of feeling part of the whole circle of existence. She didn't want to lose that connection. Not for anything.

Michael knew all of that. Yet, he was determined in his ambition. Of course, he was aware of all of the obstacles they were facing, but he believed in his dream. After all, it was her dream too, he thought. She kept him in there all of her life. She allowed him to find her. He loved her for it. He loved her eternally, but he thought that the world we lived in would never get this far without dreams. It was made of dreams and dreams turned into reality.

Another weekend passed and Maria didn't come to Faro. She kept talking to Michael online for long hours all weekend, but this time she didn't say why she wasn't coming. Michael didn't ask.

One more week passed. Michael noticed that during that week Maria was avoiding him online. They spoke just a couple of times for a few minutes. She would just ask him, "How are you?" and then she would stay quiet. Michael would ask her, "Is everything okay? What is bothering you, Maria?"

Her answer would be short, "Nothing." Then she would get quiet again. He knew that she was thinking about their relationship and he wanted to give her time. He didn't want to bother her. The following Friday she didn't talk to Michael at all, so he thought she would not come again, but then around seven o'clock in the evening a phone rang.

"I am at the train station in Portimao, just getting on the train. I will be in Faro at the usual time. Wait for me at the station, please."

Chapter Nineteen
The Last Weekend

"Once in a while, people swore that they saw Ama coming down to the gorge to drink water from Amo's spring. But those were only stories. People like fairytales."

Michael was at the train station just at the moment the train arrived. Maria walked out of the train. She didn't look very happy. They walked back to the apartment and on the way she didn't say a word. When they arrived, she left her bag in the bedroom and went to the terrace. Michael brought two glasses of wine and set them next to her.

"Michael. I came to pick up my stuff that I have here. I don't think this will work. It was mistake. It was mistake that you came to Faro. I was alone all of my life. I am used to being alone. I love you, but for me being in a dream with you is enough. And I am not even sure if you are the man from my dream. You are tainted Michael. You already have a mark. I cannot live with it."

Michael expected she was going to say something like that.

"Maria, I came to Faro to be close to you and I gave you a promise of eternal love. That will never change. I am not asking anything in return. Never was. But I feel that my soul is with you and I need to stay close to my soul. If you don't want to be in a relationship with me, it is your choice. But don't break the connection between us. Allow me to stay close. If not as your man, then as your friend. I can be your best friend. I am your best friend already and want to always stay close to you and for you whenever you need me. Without any conditions Maria."

She looked at Michael, sighed deeply and said, "Oh, I am not sure that we can even be friends. You are just saying that. You will always want a relationship. I don't know if that would work."

"Yes, it would. I love you Maria, always will and I know how to be a faithful friend."

Michael walked into the living room and came back with a few sheets of paper in his hand. "Look, I wrote short story last week. I haven't written in a long me and then it just came to me last week. I would like it if you would read this and tell me what you think." He handed her papers and she started reading.

"Amo's Gorge - A Story About the Last Unicorn"

The unicorn is a legendary animal that has been described since antiquity as a horse-like animal with a large, pointed, spiraling horn sticking out from its forehead. It was usually described as a very wild forest creature, a symbol of purity, grace, and independence, which could only be captured by a virgin. It was believed in the old times that its horn had the power to turn poisoned water drinkable and to heal sickness. According to the legend, there were many unicorns inhabiting the earth centuries ago, but slowly, under the advance and pressure of the human civilization, they disappeared.

In the mountains of Southern Portugal, somewhere in the region of Alentejo, there is a ravine called "Amo's gorge." I was there some time ago and heard from the locals the story about the last unicorn called Amo. According to the story, there were really two unicorns. Male Amo and female Ama, but nobody could tell me what happened to Ama. Some believe that she is still somewhere around running through forests and over the meadows. At least, that is what the legend says.

This is how the story goes: Some three hundred years ago, there were two last unicorns left in the world. Male called Amo and female called Ama. They really didn't know each other because they inhabited different lands, but they felt each other's existence. Often, they would dream of each other and felt some strange longing, like they belonged together. But, life was going on and they lived their lives separately never expecting that they would ever meet.

Ama was a young unicorn, happy with her being, proud of her independence and freedom. She often looked at other animals wondering why they allowed humans to tame them and use them. She couldn't understand them. She enjoyed every bit of nature that surrounded her. She loved wild flowers, cold streams, deep and mysterious woods, sounds of wind in the trees, and the music of birds. She could only feel complete feeling the land, roaming over mountains and through valleys. She felt the wholeness of creation. She knew that she was one of the most majestic living creatures still around and she was proud of it.

Once in a while, humans would see her running over lands and they admired her beauty and grace. Of course, they wanted to catch her and tame her, but she would never allow that. She enjoyed their admiration and liked to play with them. She really enjoyed the attention they were giving her. So, sometimes, Ama would even let some humans come close and touch her, manipulating their senses, just so they could feel that she was real and not a dream. Then she would run away, leaving them wondering what happened, and often, leaving them sad for the missed opportunity to catch such a precious animal.

She wasn't sure what she felt about people, but she was sure that she never wanted to give up her freedom and the wholeness and happiness that she felt running aimlessly through the wilderness. It was who she was, and she didn't want to change, not for any- thing in the world.

On the other side, in a completely other part of the world, lived Amo. He was a different story. Like Ama, being a unicorn, he loved all the same things and was proud of his independence and freedom.

He was quite older than Ama, but still a very strong male unicorn. But being male, he always had a need to prove his strength and superiority over other animals. He always needed a recognition for who he was. Especially from humans.

Occasionally, he would allow them to catch him and make them believe that they tamed him. For a while he would work on their fields, pull their carriages, run in the horse races, and do everything they asked from him, just to show his superiority and strength and to enjoy admiration by humans. But then, he would get bored by it and run away always leaving damage behind him. He would knock down barns, break fences, run over crops he was working on, pull out vines, always wanting to show to humans that he can't be used, wanting them to pay for the belief that he could be tamed. Then he would run free over lands until the next time he would allow humans to catch him.

Over time the word spread around among humans of Amo and many very angry humans were trying to catch him and punish him for the damage he was always leaving behind him. Some were even claiming that he was not a real unicorn, but just a wild horse who deserved to be put down. For them, unicorns were gracious beings, who would never acted like him. Amo didn't care about their opinion. He knew who he was and continued running through life the same way.

After many years, he got tired of the game he played and decided to settle somewhere where nobody knew him, in different part of the world, so he could avoid humans forever. He came to the mountains of Alentejo, not knowing that he moved to the lands that Ama was inhabiting.

One morning, he was standing on a high ridge, enjoying the warmth of the early morning sun, when suddenly in the distance he saw Ama running over the fields. He couldn't believe his eyes. She was the most beautiful creature he ever saw. She was the one from his dreams. His heart started pounding fast. She saw him too. Ama was equally excited, but cautious. On one side, she was happy to see another unicorn. He was a bit old, but still appeared strong and handsome. She was asking herself if it were possible that he was the one whose existence she sensed all her life. She wasn't sure if she should come closer. She was always afraid of being disappointed.

Amo ran to her direction. He was running fast, trying to impress her and show his strength. For a while, they were running parallel, but in the distance examining each other. By each mile, Amo was coming closer and closer. Ama was still afraid, but she was allowing him to shorten their distance. In the evening they came to the same meadow. They were drinking water from the same spring carefully observing each other.

Finally, Amo came to Ama. She wasn't moving. She just looked at him. They could hear each other's heart. He touched her. They laid next to each other with their bodies touching. It was a glorious feeling for both of them. A sense of completion. Of dreams come true.

In the morning, they woke up and continued running and walking through the woods enjoying the surroundings and more than anything, enjoying each other. Ama was really happy. At last, a real unicorn was next to her, somebody that could understand her. Somebody that would not try to tame her. Somebody to share in the joy of freedom and of creation without limits and without conditions. Somebody of the same kind. She couldn't believe that it would ever have happened, but it seemed that it was right here, in front of her eyes. She still had her doubts, being all her life by herself, the only unicorn. But he was here, strong and true.

Amo was also happy. He promised never to leave her side. He thought that he would always be there for her, but Ama didn't want him to be there for her, but with her. She never felt that she needed any protection or help. She was strong enough and wise enough to care for herself. She wanted to be with Amo as two equal independent beings, respecting and enjoying each other's freedom. She wanted to share the greatness of her pure love, the experiences of nature. She wanted to be enriched by the presence of the same soul, not restricted or slowed down by it. She wanted to share the affection for the things they both cherished.

Well, Amo knew what Ama wanted. He wanted the same thing, but the time he spent around humans changed him a little. On one hand, he wanted to run with Ama to the end of time, and enjoy their togetherness in the freedom of open fields, forests and mountains. On the other hand, he also wanted to have a place that would be their home.

Somewhere, where they could settle and feel the warmth of their togetherness.

The home that he was thinking about was a human category. For unicorns, home was the whole of universe. Space without boundaries. That was what Ama called home. Anyway, Amo was persistent. He took her to the ridge he discovered. He wanted to make a garden for her, full of different fruits and plants. She looked at him thinking that he was playing a childish game. Why would unicorns ever want a small garden to work in when the world was a huge garden ready to be explored. Nevertheless, for a while, she enjoyed in planning, even helping him make the garden.

Yes, she was thinking, maybe once in a while, they could stop there and rest, but for her settling somewhere was an impossible thing, something that she thought she would never enjoy. Amo failed to realize that she wanted an equally independent and free uni- corn. Somebody that she can admire for his freedom. She wanted to give him her love, but she didn't want to sacrifice her liberty. It was not the nature of unicorns. She would be unhappy forever and she didn't want him to sacrifice anything for their love and togetherness either.

Amo was of a different mind. He thought if he settled down, and built a home, that she would join him. Too many years spent with the humans had blurred his mind. He was thinking like the humans. So, he sacrificed his freedom and settled on the ridge. He wanted to show Ama that he would sacrifice anything for her love, even the freedom of a unicorn. He was waiting for her patiently.

Ama would come once in a while and spend time with Amo. She truly loved him and she hoped that he would realize his true nature and continue to run around with her as unicorns should, and forget those ideas of home.

But Amo was persistent and kept remaining on the ridge. She was getting less and less excited to go there. It was just a ridge, one of many in the mountains of Alentejo. She was losing her patience with Amo. She couldn't understand how a true unicorn could act like a human. A true unicorn would never sacrifice his freedom, not even for love. Freedom is a part of true love. For unicorns, love was an unconditional category. She actually saw his sacrifice as a weakness, something that made him lose her respect and not gain her love. She heard some of the stories that humans were spreading around about Amo, and sometimes, she was asking herself, 'What kind of unicorn would ever act like that?' Maybe he is really some wild horse pretending to be a unicorn. Is it possible that she made a mistake about him? One day, she couldn't look at him like that anymore. He didn't appear as the unicorn from her dreams. She almost felt sorry for him. That was not Amo that she first met, the fast and strong unicorn running with her shoulder to shoulder. She told him she would not come back anymore to the ridge and that everything was a mistake. And she left. She was disappointed and hurt, but she knew that nothing would lower her spirits once she was back running over open fields and through deep woods. It was the open air of the high mountains that made her feel alive. For her, it was better if Amo remained as he was, just in her dreams.

Amo stayed on the ridge feeling sorry for himself and for the lost love of Ama. He couldn't believe that she really left him. He neglected his garden and soon he had no food left. He didn't eat for days. He didn't want to eat. He didn't want to live. He didn't care about anything anymore. All he was thinking was how he needed Ama. Finally, he realized what a big mistake he made. All she wanted from him was to be who he was, a true unicorn. He was angry with himself for acting like a human. How could he be so stupid?

As he was laying for days on the ridge, humans from the valley who were trying to find him and punish him, noticed him there. They started advancing up the hill, getting more and more eager to make him pay for his bad deeds. He looked at them approaching. He wasn't sure if he wanted to run or stay there and wait for his destiny, but something inside him told him that he should jump and run. That he should try to be a true unicorn. Maybe one day, it didn't matter when, Ama would meet him again. He will show her that he is the one: a true unicorn. He was the unicorn from her dreams.

He stood up slowly. He couldn't go down the hill. Humans were closing in on his escape route. The only way was to jump from the ridge to another ridge over the deep ravine. He looked at the distance. He used to jump further than that before. He would make it, he thought. Then he jumped. But his muscles were weak and his body wasn't what it used to be. Days spent laying down without food and water took their toll on him. He didn't make it to the next ridge. He fell into a deep ravine and died there.

Humans came to the edge of the ridge looking down at his motionless and bloody body. One of them said, "Well, they were right. After all, he was not a unicorn, just a wild horse who met his deserved destiny. A real unicorn would jump this distance."

Years later, at the place he fell, a spring broke out from the rock with an abundance of extremely pure and fresh water. Local people were talking about the magical properties of the water that was healing many illnesses. Some local people remembered that a unicorn fell and died there and connected those two things, so they named the spring, " Amo's Spring" and they named the gorge, "Amo's Gorge." Some say, it was just as he would want it. He always craved human recognition. Now, he finally had it forever. Once in a while, people swore that they saw Ama coming down to the gorge to drink water from Amo's spring. But those were only stories. People like fairytales.

Maria finished reading Michael's short story, raised her eyes, looked at him and said with sadness in her voice, "Yeah, this is us, this story is about us."

"I don't want that to be our story," Michael said. "I respect your independence. I respect the way you strive for your freedom and I will never try to constrain you in any way, but I will never stop loving you, Maria. No matter what you say or what you do, I will always keep my promise."

Maria stood up and then sat in Michael's lap. She hugged him, looked at his face for a few seconds and then said, "You are my Romanian rascal and I love you, Michael." They kissed.

Their kiss was long and passionate. Then they went to the bedroom and made love into the morning.

§

During that weekend, everything seemed as normal as before. They took long walks around Faro, cooked together, watched movies and made love. On Sunday morning she cleaned the bathroom, did laundry and ironed Michael's shirts. They never spoke about Michael's problems. Michael thought that she had changed her mind and that everything would be as it was before.

In the afternoon, she started packing the clothing that she kept in the apartment. Michael looked at her.

"Why are you taking all of your clothing?"

"Oh, I just have too many things over here. I want to wash them at home. I will bring some when I come next time.

Michael didn't like that. But he didn't want to comment any more.

Chapter Twenty
Mercy and Grace

"My friend, hope is our biggest enemy. It does not bring realization. It just prolongs suffering."

Five weeks passed since Maria's last visit. Weekend after weekend Michael was hoping that she would come, but she didn't. They would speak online once in a while. But most of the time, she would be online and she would see that Michael was there as well, and she wouldn't say anything. Michael was hurting, but he didn't want to press her. He never wanted to initiate the conversation. He was waiting for her.

The apartment felt empty without Maria and her things. Michael's financial situation was bad. Except for two small projects, work was not coming from New York and he didn't have any motivation to call people and ask for more work. He felt like he was losing his strength and his will to live. He didn't have money to pay his rent again and his landlord was a bit upset, but he agreed to wait.

Michael borrowed small amounts of money from Francisco again. His neighbor felt that Michael was in trouble and he didn't even bother asking him when was he going to repay his debt. Michael still owed him first four hundred.

The last week in July, just as Michael was thinking about what to do in order to get some work and continue living in Faro, Maria sent him a message on Skype:

"You are a deceiver and liar Michael. All of your life you were deceiving people. You deceived me too. How could I be so stupid not to see that. You are just like a sick old dog in heat chasing after young women. I hate you."

That was all. Michael looked at the message and he couldn't believe it. He tried to call her on Skype and by phone, but she wouldn't answer. The next day, Maria deleted her name as a friend and contact from all Michael's accounts online—Facebook, Goodreads, Skype, Google mail, and iMessage.

Few days later, Carlos came from Lisbon on business to Faro and he met Michael in a café near Michael's apartment.

"Bom dia," Carlos said. "How are you today?"

"Bom dia, Carlos," Michael answered. "I don't know. Just having a coffee and feeling sorry for myself."

"Why? That is not a very useful thing. Doesn't solve anything," Carlos said.

Michael told him in short about the happy times he spent with Maria and about the way everything ended after she learned about his past.

"I just kept asking myself where I made a mistake. For years I was searching for her and finally I had found her. That first weekend I thought I was at the last door and all I had to do was knock and it would be open to me. The King with the key. But the doors didn't open. I remained in front of it, hoping it would, week after week, but nothing happened. If I don't have hope, I don't know how I would live and go on day after day."

"You say, you can't live without hope? My friend, hope is our biggest enemy. It does not bring realization. It just prolongs suffering." Carlos kept talking. "You know, when Pandora opened her box and released all the evils of mankind, the only one remaining in the box was hope. And since then, hope keeps flirting and deceiving human souls. People say that hope is an emotional state opposite of despair. But in reality hope triggers despair. You are now in despair, my friend, and you wouldn't be if all you were doing, wasn't just hoping."

"But for me, Carlos," Michael said, "hope is essential in searching for the higher meaning of life, when one is on the path often covered with mist of the unknown before him. Faith in the unseen and hope of finding it is what moved pilgrims for centuries in their discoveries, without any expectation of reward other than the understanding of our inner nature and the creation."

Carlos smiled and kept talking. "There is something called positive thinking that people often confuse with hope. But it is different. Positive thinking is a state of mind, while hope is a useless state of the heart. Positive thinking is about doing and hope is about feeling. So, positive thinking is what you need."

"Yes, but what should I do?" Michael asked. "For three months everything seemed flawless. It felt like a completion of an alchemical process with all of the right elements coming together in perfect harmony and then after that, nothing."

"So, you just mentioned the answer yourself. Positive thinking, in your case, would mean trying to recreate the same conditions that you had during that time. Think about the elements that were there, about the conditions. Think about what brought the feeling of perfect completion. Work on those elements. Make them stronger. Work on those conditions. Make them permanent. Chemical processes are a sensitive matter. You have to keep all of the tools and vessels you are using clean at all times. Even if you have the right elements and conditions, the dirt of the vessels would corrupt the process, without you ever noticing. And the way I see you, you are sitting and hoping, and the dirt in your alchemical laboratory is piling up and it will be harder and harder for you to get anywhere like that."

"But I don't know how to recreate that process. It took me years of work, going through different phases to come to here. I know I am at the right place, yet nothing is working right."

"You know, when I was a kid I wasn't very good in math." Carlos continued like he didn't hear Michael's comment at all. "And I had a good teacher. She was maybe in her thirties, but she looked much younger. All of the boys in school were in love with her, including me. Sometimes I was even happy that I wasn't doing things correctly because she would spend time with me trying to explain the right way and how to get to the correct result of a math problem. But most often, I wouldn't listen, I would just stare at her. Nevertheless, I remember one thing. If you have a math problem to solve and you fill up pages and pages with different calculations and at the end, you come up with a wrong result, the only way to find a mistake is to go back to the beginning and re-check your calculations. She used to tell me, Carlos, you showed that you were working hard, but the result is wrong. You made a mistake. You have to go back to the beginning. So, pretty much, I have the same advice for you. You claim that you had the perfect result, but you really don't know how you got there. In order to find if it was the right result, how you came to the perfection you are mentioning, you have to go back to your beginning, wherever that was."

Carlos always had smart words of advice. After they finished their coffee, Carlos gave Michael one hundred Euros. "Here, you may need this. You will give it back to me whenever you want." Then, he left. Michael stayed there thinking about his words. In many ways, he was right.

Where to go? What to do? Michael didn't know. He felt stuck. He felt stuck within himself. His mind, his soul, his heart, and his body all felt stuck. He knew that we all are our own creations. We are what we think and what we believe. And now all of his thoughts and all of his beliefs were frozen in that first weekend in Faro. He wanted it to last forever, but it was over and nothing seemed good afterward.

He went home. His home didn't feel warm anymore. He knew why. Before he knew how to be happy anywhere with anybody, at any place, because his true home was always in himself. But at that moment, he felt like he placed his home in somebody else's soul and that soul wasn't there. So, he felt misplaced in the place he lived. He had to do something. He had to regain his home. He lost himself. He had to regain himself.

Carlos was right, Michael thought. He had to go back to the beginning. But where was the beginning? He decided that he should go back to New York. He called Carlos and asked him if he would get him a ticket from Lisbon to New York. Carlos agreed. An hour latter, Michael received confirmation email for the flight next day at noon.

§

Early next morning, he packed up just his backpack with his laptop and the notebook Maria gave him for his birthday. He left everything else. He placed apartment keys in the envelope and left in the mailbox for his landlord. He was planning to send him an email from New York. Michael didn't know what was he going to say to his landlord, but he was going to think about that later. He took the first train to Lisbon and then a cab to the airport, checked in and went straight to the passport control. He spent a few minutes waiting while a border policeman was checking his passport. Then the policeman turned the page and stamped it.

Michael continued walking to the terminal. 'My life is falling apart again,' he thought. He raised his head up and whispered, "Mercy, oh

Lord, mercy." He felt very tired. Then another thought came to his mind: 'God gave me so much grace in last couple of years, and here I am again asking for mercy. When will this madness stop?'

Chapter Twenty-One
The Return

"Coming so close to the realization of my dreams and trying to turn my dreams into reality without success, left me torn apart between the world of dreams and reality."

Michael arrived at the Newark Airport at four o'clock in the afternoon. He walked out of the terminal building looking for a bus to Manhattan. With only fifty dollars in his pocket and not a place to go, it was a repetition of his last return to New York, when he ended up in the Bowery Mission, a shelter for homeless.

As the bus was making a turn towards the entrance into Lincoln Tunnel, Michael could see across the Hudson River the panorama of the city. 'Another failure, another fight for survival,' he said to himself. He felt defeated. He felt that all of his life was spent in vain. 'That is so sad,' he thought.

Once in Manhattan, he walked straight to the Bowery Mission.

At the entrance of the Bowery Mission, he bumped into Keith, the Mission Director. Keith was a young, vibrant man who came to the Bowery Mission as a homeless person himself and remained there to work and rose to the position of director. He was very kind and straight forward - a well-liked person by all homeless men in Manhattan.

"Good afternoon, Director."

"Hi, Michael. How are you? Haven't see you in a few months. Is it everything okay?" Director asked and looked at Michael with curiosity.

"Well, not exactly Director…" Michael said with the heaviness in his voice.

"Why? What happened Michael?" Director asked and place his hand on the Michael's shoulder, "Tell me."

"I am back. I messed up my life again, Director. I am so ashamed. I need a place to stay," he said after a deep sigh.

"I am sorry to hear that, Michael, but it happens. You are neither the first nor the last one. Many men come back to the Mission several times before they manage to finally live on their own. You should not be ashamed. We will find a place for you here. You will regain your strength again. Come with me upstairs to the reception office."

Michael signed up again for a six-month recovery program in the Bowery Mission. Director Keith decided to be his counselor. "I don't know if you knew that, but your old counselor, Pastor Charles, was transferred to our new facility in Harlem. It is better for him. It's closer to his home and he is going to retire soon any way. So I am going to be your counselor."

Director Keith and Michael spent many hours talking about Michael's life. He wasn't a typical homeless man that participated in a program. Most of them were alcoholics or drug addicts and their reasons for becoming homeless were obvious. His reasons were unusual and deeper. And sometimes they were far above and over anything that Pastor Keith could apprehend, regardless of the rich experience he had in dealing with men in the recovery program.

Michael's moods were changing from day to day. Sometimes he was upbeat and full of energy. Other days he would be sad and on the verge of crying. In one of the sessions he spoke about his dreams.

"You know," he started, "the reason I failed in my attempt to get close to Maria was not my past. Both of us were dreamers, but she was still asleep and I was dreaming awake. I could not wake her up. She was afraid to wake up with somebody who was dreaming awake. Dreaming awake is sometimes a dangerous thing. In trying to get to heaven you may end up in the hell. "

"So, why don't you stop dreaming awake? You have to learn to control you dreams." Director said.

"It is easier to say than to do so. Coming so close to the realization of my dreams and trying to turn my dreams into reality without success, left me torn apart between the world of dreams and reality."

"Did you ever think that you are dreaming so much because you are trying to avoid to face reality. Are you afraid of anything? Are you afraid of reality? You told to Pastor Charles once that you would like to have a new beginning in life with this new woman you were chasing after in Portugal. Why do you want so much this new beginning? Do you think that the new beginning will postpone the end? Are you afraid of the end? Are you afraid of death Michael?"

"No, Director. For me, death represents just another voyage. The natural continuation of things according to God's master plan. Death in itself is not sad or tragic. It is the sense of separation and loss that remain with those who stay behind in the world of living that brings sorrow. It is the same like with the falling tree in the forest. If nobody was there to hear it falling, did it make noise? If one departs this life and nobody was around to feel sorry, does that makes death tragic? No, it's just another voyage in the great adventure called Creation.One day he came to Director's office with the little black notebook in his hands.

"Once in a while, I look at a little notebook that she gave me. I know that everything in there is the truth. I also know that I was not the only seeker of the Holy Grail.

"Holy Grail? What is for you the Holy Grail?" Director asked.

"It is the unconditional love thought to us by our Teacher from Nazareth. Red Rose plucked from the Garden in Heavens to be sacrificed for the sake of the ultimate lesson. One day, somebody will be worthy enough to fulfil the mission. All that is left for me are my memories— the weekend in Faro, when I was so close to it and so happy and so in love." – He started crying. He slammed his fist into Director's desk, moaned loudly, jumped, and ran out of the office. That was the only time Director saw him cry.

Most of the days, Michael would spend in the Mission Chapel meditating and praying or in the computer room writing. When Director asked him what was he writing about, he said: "About the eighth door. Many years ago, a friend of mine told me to be careful when going through the eighth door. It is the one before the last and final, ninth door. The Eighth door is a revolving door. I would have to go straight through, not thinking about words. But I made a mistake. I was thinking about words and I kept spinning around. That is what brought me here. When I was back in Faro, I lived on the seventh floor. It was a sign for me that I passed seven doors and that I am in front the eighth door. But I failed. I didn't pay attention. I didn't see that as a sign. But it will not happen again."

Director didn't understand the meaning of what Michael was talking about, but he didn't want to ask further.

Director Keith read carefully Michael's old file and counselor's notes. He spoke with Pastor Charles on the phone several times after sessions with Michael. He consulted with Pastor Paul who was very close to Michael last time Michael was in the Bowery Mission. He spoke with Michael's friends and with his ex-wife. He tried to understand Michael and help with advice, but after a few sessions he gave up on that idea. It was obvious that Michael's mind was already set with what he was after in recovery program. The Bowery Mission was just a break for him. The way to regain his strength back and continue with whatever he was after. Men like him never gave up. So at the regular sessions with Michael, Director would just sit and listen to what Michael wanted to say.

Then one morning, just as Director arrived in his office, Michael ran in all excited. He had his backpack with him.

"Listen, I am leaving. I have to go home. It is time. You have to sign my discharge papers"

"Hold on, slow down. Where are you going? Which home? Are you leaving the program? Sit down and tell me what happened?"

"Okay. I will, but I don't have too much time. It is time. The doors will close if I don't rush," he said, he sat down, then continued. "I was up all of last night in the Chapel praying. There was nobody else there but me. And then in the middle of the night I had a visit. Archangel Michael came to me again and spoke to me. He told me that Gods decided that my punishments in this world are over. I paid for my crimes. My soul is restored as a pure soul of a righteous man. I will be able to dream my dream again. I will be able to go to the world of dreams and be with my Love again. Isn't that great?"

"Yes, Michael, that is great. But what about this world? What will you do when you walk out of here? Where will you go?" Director asked.

"That is not important, man. Wherever I go, whatever I do, it will be a success. Nothing can happen to me anymore. I am under protection. "

"Whose protection Michael?" – Director asked.

"The one who taught me to love others as I love myself and to do unto others as I would want them to do unto me. Now I can do that. My punishment is over. I am a free man.

Then, he left. Keith wanted to stop him from leaving, but the Mission counselors don't have that authority. For a while, he worried that Michael did something stupid like jump off the bridge or walk off of the roof like his friend Chris, but Keith hadn't heard anything. If something like that happened, he was sure he would hear about it.

§

It was nine thirty Thursday morning when Michael entered the lobby of the National Library of Portugal in Lisbon. He sat on the sofa opposite of the security desk. 'Carlos should come soon. He is never late,' he thought.

Carlos entered into the lobby, approached and sat next to Michael. He was in his office in the Santa Maria hospital all morning and didn't have time to change. He was still in his whites.

"Olá Michael.

"Hi Carlos. Thank you for coming. You are a real friend."

"Listen Michael. I don't know why I am doing this. Everybody is saying bad things about you. Wherever you go, whatever you do, there is a noise after you. If I tell our Masonic friends in New York that I am helping you, they would say I am crazy. In spite of everything, I respect your courage to go after your ideals, no matter what. Men like you make this world spin around. I know that the road you chose to go is covered with thorns. But I also know that it must be a road to the stars. So, I brought you money that you ask for. If you are careful, it will last you for three months. I am sure you can find a room in Lisbon for two hundred a month. So try to manage. It is my gift to you. No need to repay me ever. If you ever get in a position to think about repaying me, give instead a donation to some animal shelter in my name. And please, don't call me any time soon to get you another ticket to New York," Carlos started smiling here, "In last three months I bought you two tickets already. Or maybe, just give me enough notice in advance so I could find a good deal, ha, ha."

"Not to worry Carlos. This time I have everything figured out."

"I really hope so. You are expensive friend to have Michael. So what did you figure out?"

"I figured out where the key to my purpose is."

"Where it is?" Carlos asked.

"Right here." Michael said.

"Here? In this Library?" Carlos asked.

"Yes. Or better to say, this is where the key will unlock the door of my purpose."

"I am not sure if I understand you? Carlos asked.

"Don't you see? I was going after a woman believing that the key is in being with her. But the key is in writing about her. The key is in words that are in me. Longing for her is just an impulse for words to come out. And the whole purpose is for words to come out. Words are important. Words about love. Words about life. And they are not mine. They are just channeled through me. Remember, in the beginning there was the word, and the word was with God, and the word was God, and the word was made flesh. The whole purpose of all my life was to accumulate enough impulse for all the writings that need to be done. That is my mission. That is the Holy Grail I was after. There is so much despair in the world today. People are losing fate in God. Nobody believes in love anymore Carlos. Nobody. Hope, Love, and Kindness are today only empty phrases from the Sunday Bible school. People need love. They need hope. Hope of the Rose. But before they understand what hope of the Rose represents, they need to hear truth. Truth is important."

"Truth according to Michael?" Carlos said.

"Yes…according to Michael. It could be also according to Carlos, according to Maria, according to anybody. Name doesn't matter. But in each of us is a little bit of Michael, ha, ha," Michael said, "and some don't like me because they recognize themselves in me. My truth belongs to all."

"And I assume this is where you are going to write it? Carlos asked while pointing at the entrance of the reading room.

"Yes. I love this space. I can sit here in the reading room surrounded with books and write all day. It is so quiet and inspiring. They have wi-fi. And it is free." Michael smiled.

"And young girls from the Lisbon University writing their school papers next to you." Carlos said with a bit of irony in his voice while shaking his head.

"Yes, I was thinking about the same thing. Isn't that nice ha, ha. But it won't make difference to me. I'll be with my Maria."

"Whoever that is…" Carlos said and smiled.

§

About a year later, in New York, Director Keith was passing by the Barnes and Noble book store on Union Square. He saw a familiar face on a poster in the store window. It was an announcement of the book signing, *Truth According to Michael* by Michael Nicolau." He smiled and continued walking. 'Yes, Michael was right - he was under protection,' Director was thinking, 'I wonder if Michael ever passed through the eighth door…I'll ask him. I'll go to that book signing and ask him.'

About the Author

Stevan V. Nikolic was born in Belgrade, Serbia in 1958 and moved to New York, USA in 1987. He began his literary career as a poet before turning to non-fiction and fiction.

As a writer, he spent last thirty-five years studying various forms of esoteric spirituality. Mr. Nikolic is the author of nine nonfiction and two fiction books published in English, Serbian, Portuguese, and Spanish language: *Royal Art* (2006), *The Peace of the Rose* (2007) *The Purpose of Freemasonry* (2008), *Freemasonry in Serbia* (2011), *On the Square–Decoding Freemasonry* (2013) , *Spiritual Guide to the Secret of Birth* - a four books series written in Serbian language, on Astrology, Alchemy, Kabbalah, and Ancient Mysteries (2010/2011), and novels *Weekend in Faro* (2014) and *Truth According To Michael* (2016).

To learn more about Stevan V. Nikolic visit: **stevanvnikolic.com**

www.ingramcontent.com/pod-product-compliance
Lightning Source LLC
Chambersburg PA
CBHW032036180726
48284CB00008B/2607